DARK TIMES

Dark Times

Edited by
Ann Walsh

RONSDALE PRESS

DARK TIMES
Copyright © 2005 held by the authors herein

RONSDALE PRESS
3350 West 21st Avenue
Vancouver, B.C., Canada V6S 1G7
www.ronsdalepress.com

Typesetting: Julie Cochrane, in Minion 12 pt on 16
Cover Art: Mark Swiecki, photographer
Cover Design: Julie Cochrane
Paper: Ancient Forest Friendly Rolland "Enviro" — 100% post-consumer
    waste, totally chlorine-free and acid-free

Ronsdale Press wishes to thank the Canada Council for the Arts, the Government of Canada through the Book Publishing Industry Development Program (BPIDP), and the Province of British Columbia through the British Columbia Arts Council for their support of its publishing program.

Library and Archives Canada Cataloguing in Publication

Dark times / editor: Ann Walsh.

ISBN 1-55380-028-1

1. Death — Juvenile fiction. 2. Grief — Juvenile fiction.
3. Youth and death — Juvenile fiction. 4. Children's stories, Canadian (English). I. Walsh, Ann, 1942–.

PS8323.D37D37 2005   jC813'.010806   C2005-904246-X

Printed in Canada by Hignell Printing

Contents

Introduction

ANN WALSH

. . .

Loss is one of the earliest — and the hardest — of life's lessons. The puppy that is run over on the highway, the kitten that becomes ill and has to be put to "sleep" and even the frog scooped from the lake who lies still and lifeless in our pudgy toddler hands — experiences such as these are often our first exposure to the agony of loss.

But a loss does not always mean a death. There are many other ways of losing something or someone we love.

For most of us, the first person in our lives that we lose is a grandparent. Two of the stories in this book, "Sisters" and "All is Calm," are about such a loss. One deals with the death of a grandparent; in the other story it is the mind of the grandmother that has gone, lost to Alzheimer's disease.

Our parents are older than we are, so it stands to reason they will probably die before we do. We may not think about this very often; in our hearts, however, we know it is true. In "The Canoe," a story set on the West Coast of Vancouver Island, a First Nations father and son confront each other as they work through their grief for the wife and mother whose death they mourn.

In the stories "Cold Snap" and "Dear Family," the parents are still alive, although they are very much "lost" to their children.

Sometimes brothers and sisters die, but we can lose them in other ways, too. The stories "Snow Angel" and "A Few Words for My Brother" are about young people who lost the battle for a normal life before they ever had one — they were born with Fetal Alcohol Syndrome. The brother and sister in these two stories could not be kept safe, even though they were armoured by the love of their adoptive families.

Two of the stories in this book are about the death of a school friend. In "Hang On" a young boy visits with the parents of his injured friend and tries to offer them comfort. In "Kick" the classroom bully has died, and one of his victims must deal with the confusing emotions that death leaves in its wake.

Sometimes we see the loss coming, and we do everything we can to prevent it. Such is the case in "Explaining Andrew," a story about a young man trying desperately to help his schizophrenic older brother. But that brother, the person he was before he became ill, no longer exists. He has been replaced by someone who is physically the same but whose every thought and action have been changed by the disease.

The death of a small child brings with it one of the darkest of times. In "the sign for heaven" the loss of the child to whom she is teaching sign language shakes the faith of a young girl as she wonders why God would let a child die.

"Dreams in a Pizza Box" is the story of young people who lose both their only parent and their home. Their lives change drastically with this loss and only a few carefully stored mementoes remain of what was once a family.

Almost everyone who grieves goes through several predictable stages before emerging from the darkness. In "Balance Restored" we watch a young girl as she makes her way, slowly, through these stages.

These stories are all about dark times. But, as in real life, the darkness lifts. It sometimes is hard to believe, but eventually time works its magic and the healing begins. We still miss what we have lost, but we no longer mourn so violently. Eventually, all grief gentles.

Perhaps this book will help others find their way out of the dark times and into the sunlight.

Snow Angel

BY CAROLYN POGUE

. . .

Elizabeth Ann arrived on the shortest day of the year during a wicked snow storm. Her mom blasted in with her and then stood on the door mat blinking in the bright light. Elizabeth Ann wore a yellow and white snow suit. Her long black eye lashes glistened with melting snow. Her mom looked messy, like she'd got dressed in a hurry. She hadn't brushed her hair and she wasn't wearing a hat or boots, even though the snow was deep. She smelled of alcohol.

Elizabeth Ann's mom is my aunt but we hardly ever saw her. She steered clear of us most of the time. We all lived in Yellowknife, which is not a huge city, but we never visited her. She burst in, didn't knock or anything, just opened the kitchen door and stood there. We were finishing dinner.

"What are you looking at?" she demanded, stamping the snow off her runners. "It's just us. Just family. Thought we'd pay you a Christmas visit." My mom stood up, staring at her younger sister. Mom's face moved between gladness and shock. "Come in, honey," she said, and went to hug her.

My aunt pushed Elizabeth Ann toward her. "Hey," she said, "I actually need a little favour. Just 'til I get on my feet again." Her eyes glistened but she stuck her chin up and clamped her jaw tight to stop it from shaking. "Just 'til I get on my feet again," she repeated.

She touched Elizabeth Ann's cheek with the back of her fingers. "You be a good girl for your auntie." Then she turned and ran out the door. There was deafening silence at first, then Mom asked, "Mary, could you close the door, please?" When I did, I found the suitcase on the porch. That was the last we ever saw of my aunt. She just disappeared. Mom thinks she went to Edmonton or maybe Vancouver.

Elizabeth Ann was four years old when she arrived, half my age. She had wavy black hair, big eyes and a deep belly laugh. "What a big laugh for a little kid!" people said, and they'd laugh, too. For a while, anyway. The other thing that people said was, "My! She sure is a *busy* little girl!" which meant, "Couldn't you get her to sit still and be quiet for five minutes?" It seemed that Elizabeth Ann had a spring inside her. She'd whirl around the house like a tornado and then suddenly you'd find her fast asleep on the floor or under a jumble of cushions on the couch. Shanti called her "Miss All or Nothing."

Shanti was the most patient with her, but Shanti is patient with everyone — including the creatures she dragged home. Shanti means "peace" in Hindi, so I guess that explains it. We adopted her when she was three years old; I was four then. Shanti was quiet. Pretty much the opposite of Elizabeth Ann.

Shanti's side of our bedroom was usually floor-to-ceiling cages, boxes and fish bowls. You never knew who'd be sharing the room with us: a sparrow that crashed into a window, a kitten with three legs, gerbils that kids didn't want anymore, goldfish saved from "the big flush." Mom said, "Eventually the unwanted and helpless seem to find their way to Shanti." Shanti nursed them to health, or buried the ones that didn't make it. She was famous for her animal funerals. You can still see the stones in the yard with her printing on them: "Rest in Peace Foofoo," things like that. What I remember is that "the tornado" calmed down when she was with Shanti and the animals. There was a gentleness in her, then.

Jessy, our older brother, liked Elizabeth Ann, as long as she stayed out of his room. He was ten when Elizabeth Ann arrived, and he was busy being a chess wizard, a boxing champion and a grade four genius. He really didn't have too much time for Shanti or me, much less a noisy little kid. If Elizabeth Ann sat still to hear a story, he'd read to her. If she wiggled, he'd close the book, sigh, and retreat to his room to get smarter than he already was.

Our mom didn't seem too fazed by having a new kid. Maybe she really believed it was temporary. She moved her home office into a corner of the kitchen and made her office into a small extra bedroom. Actually, it was like a closet, but Elizabeth Ann loved it. It was big enough for her imagination and that's all she needed.

Mom runs "Second Hand Rose," selling used clothes and moose hide mitts and mukluks that Dene women make. In the beginning, Elizabeth Ann went to the shop, just like we had before we started school. Mom had art supplies and books there to keep kids busy. But Elizabeth Ann preferred playing dress-up with shoes and clothes or talking to customers. The ones with a sense of humour kept coming back; the others came less often. They didn't think it was funny when Elizabeth Ann looked under the door of the change room and yelled, "Boo!"

Mom is a pretty ordinary mother. She loves us, which is a good thing to know, and she doesn't freak out too often. She reads, plays Scrabble and takes us camping every summer. She works on the Peace and Justice committee at church and writes letters for Amnesty International, which is all about writing to political prisoners.

I like reading, too, and writing stories. This makes me a geek at school sometimes, but mostly life is pretty ordinary. I like fishing on Great Slave Lake and at Uncle Bill's in Peace

River, Alberta, where we sometimes go for holidays. I've been in all the plays our school put on. Being able to act sure came in handy later when people asked about Elizabeth Ann. But at first it wasn't like that. At first it was really neat to have another little sister. We all took turns reading her a bedtime story. One night, she said, "I can read to you, Mary!" And she stood there proudly, holding an old dictionary upside down. Then she recited the whole story of *The Three Billy Goats Gruff,* imitating Jessy's sound effects and voices of the goats and the troll. I nearly wet my pants laughing. But she was always doing surprising things.

One morning we woke up to the scream of the smoke alarm. We followed the smoke into the kitchen and found Elizabeth Ann standing on a chair at the stove. She was five. Every element on the stove was red hot. Smoking brown butter sizzled in four frying pans. She whirled when we rushed in, wearing a big happy smile. She pointed at Mom with the spatula. "How many eggs for your breakfast, Auntie?"

When she was six, Elizabeth Ann came with me to my after-school rehearsals for a musical. By the end of a week, she'd memorized everyone's lines and all the musical numbers. At breakfast, she drilled me on my lines and then sang my solo all the way to school. During rehearsals she became the unofficial prompter; she was the only kid *not* in grade five who was named in the program. She could have been a music theatre star some day. But it isn't the star thing that I remember most. It's the angel thing.

About a week after she arrived, I remember coming home from school and finding what Mom called "a host of angels" in the yard. How cool is that? In Yellowknife, there isn't much daylight in December. We go to school in the dark, have first recess at sunrise, and watch the sun set at last recess. That day, I remember that the street lamp cast a soft light in our yard; the snow angels looked beautiful.

Elizabeth Ann was obsessed with snow angels. When the first flake hit the ground, she'd be in the basement yelling, "Where are my mitts? I need boots!" She'd struggle into her snowsuit and find someone to zip her up. Then she'd run out, fling herself into the snow and start.

Keeping her head still, she'd move her arms up and down, up and down to make the wings. If it was a girl angel, she'd move her legs back and forth to make a skirt. Ever so carefully then, Elizabeth Ann would pull herself up, take three steps forward, then turn. "There, angel," she'd announce, "now people can see you." And she would move on to the next place where the snow was free of footprints. She made snow angels for years. And then one winter she didn't. How old was she then? Ten, maybe?

That was when things began to change at home — for everybody. When Elizabeth Ann was ten, I was fourteen. I could hardly jam all my homework into my pack. Jessy the genius was representing the Territories at national boxing championships. Shanti was working after school at the animal shelter. Mom was trying to decide what to do about the shop. "I either have to expand it or close it," she said, "and I don't want to do either." Everyone was busy with life. Maybe that's why we didn't notice right away that Elizabeth Ann wasn't laughing much anymore. She wasn't making anyone else laugh, either.

It happened slowly, so that it's only in looking back that you can actually see the change. Cute and cheeky became rude. We started getting complaints from her teachers. I added a new word to my vocabulary when I overheard my friends talking about her: *obnoxious.*

When she was eleven, another complication came along. She acted like a bratty, moody kid — but her body looked about eighteen years old. That was also the year Elizabeth Ann and her friend were caught stealing cigarettes and lighters from the convenience store. After the girls paid back the store and apologized, the other mother wouldn't let the girls play together any more. She blamed it all on Elizabeth Ann's bad influence. But that year, I had my own problems.

I was fifteen and high school was hard; they piled on the homework until I could hardly see over the top of my books. I don't know how the other kids could have a social life and keep up with homework. I couldn't seem to, not that boys were falling over themselves to date me or anything. Anyway, life just seemed to get busier and rushed. Shanti went from school to the animal clinic. I went straight to the library. The genius was either at the gym or hunched over a chess board somewhere. So we just weren't paying attention when it all started to unravel.

One night Shanti and I were walking home. It was September. There was a cold wind blowing up from the lake; birch and poplar leaves swirled at our feet. Shanti was "babysitting" a neighbour's ferret. It had bad nerves or something and had licked and bitten its own foot until it bled, the way people bite their nails. We detoured to the drug store to get ointment for the poor thing, then took a short cut through the alley behind the post office. There was a knot of people there, passing around a bottle in a paper bag. We'd seen them around town before, usually in an alley, usually drinking. No big deal, we just kept walking. Until we heard her laugh.

Elizabeth Ann's eyes were shiny. She looked happy. She was smoking a cigarette. "Hey!" she said. "Look who's here! Wanna meet my new friends?"

I was stunned. I couldn't breathe. Then Shanti said gently, "Come on home, honey, dinner will be ready." In my mind, the whole scene freezes here. I look at the people around Elizabeth Ann: there were seven, all older than her, all grinning at us. "Your little sister will be home later," said a man. "Don't worry; we'll look after her." I lost it then. I grabbed Elizabeth Ann's jacket and screamed in her face. "You are coming with us *now!*" Her eyes lost their dreamy look. "Hey," said the man, "take it easy."

"*You* take it easy!" I yelled. "She's only twelve years old!" By the time we got home Shanti and Elizabeth Ann were both crying. I was too furious for tears. Elizabeth Ann went straight to bed and fell asleep instantly. When Mom got home, we called a family council. It turned out that things were worse than any of us thought.

"I was waiting for the moment to mention it," Mom said, "but three times in the last two weeks the books haven't balanced at the shop. There's money missing."

"The principal called," Jessy said. "She skipped school today. She's suspended until Monday." We decided that maybe Elizabeth Ann was alone too much, that she needed more of our attention. "Maybe I could give her boxing lessons to build up her confidence," Jessy said. "And maybe not," I said. "What if Mary and I tutored her so she can raise her marks?" Shanti offered.

The next week Elizabeth Ann skipped school again. "What's going on, Elizabeth Ann?" Mom asked that night. She sat at the kitchen table, her arms folded across her chest.

"I don't know," she said, "I just want to have fun, I guess."

"Stealing and drinking and skipping school is fun?" Mom asked.

"Not when you say it like that."

"How else could I say it?"

Elizabeth Ann scowled and clamped her jaw shut. Shanti tried next.

"We don't want you to get into trouble. You're hanging around with scary people. They'll hurt you."

Silence slipped into the kitchen like a cold draft. Jessy drummed his fingers on the table. I was mad. Why wouldn't she see the consequences of what she was doing? The silence seemed to last a long time.

"I want you to talk to someone," Mom said, "a professional who might help you feel better about yourself. All right?"

"Do whatever you want," Elizabeth Ann snapped. "I'm going to disappear." She stood up so fast her chair crashed to the floor, then ran to her room and slammed the door.

The psychologist saw her every Tuesday after school. We couldn't see much change; she still seemed angry all the time. After two months the psychologist suggested family therapy, so now we all had to show up Tuesdays. He was looking for abuse or something. What happened when she was little? How did she feel about her mother?

For that last year we all walked on egg shells waiting for the next explosion or the next expulsion. We couldn't figure out how to help Elizabeth Ann and she couldn't seem to tell us what was wrong.

One night I went into her room and asked her turn down her music. It was deafening even for me and I was only sixteen. I touched her hand. She pulled it away. "Tell me," I said, "tell me how to help you feel better." Elizabeth Ann looked up from her magazine. It seemed the tide came in bringing a look of love, and then the tide went out again, leaving the gravelly shore of anger. "Get lost," she said.

"I'll go," I said, "but . . . nothing you can do will make me stop loving you, even when I lose my temper. Do you know that?"

Elizabeth Ann said, "Disappear."

The psychologist turned us over to a psychiatrist. He talked about anger management and other stuff that made Elizabeth Ann mad, and then decided that Elizabeth Ann was depressed. "Teenage depression is common," he said, even though she wasn't a teenager yet. He prescribed anti-depressants, and we all stayed home again on Tuesday nights.

When the pills kicked in, there were more days between angry outbursts. And then, just when we thought that we could all get back to normal, Elizabeth Ann made a decision. There was no note and no farewell.

That Friday night I came home from the late movie — I was finally dating. The street lamp cast a soft light over the yard, and there it was: one single snow angel. I tiptoed into Elizabeth Ann's room to say, "Hey! It's cool to see your angel again," but she was asleep. The next morning when she didn't appear for breakfast, Jessy went into her room to see if she was all right. She wasn't.

After the ambulance took away her body, we figured out what had happened. She had climbed out her window; the tracks were there in the snow. She must have sneaked out to be with her alley friends. Then she'd come home, made the angel, climbed back in the window and swallowed all her pills.

When someone you love dies by suicide it's like being kicked in the stomach; you can't get your breath. Any part of you that doesn't hurt, is numb. When you look out and see people walking along the street or ravens sailing through the blue sky, you can hardly believe that the world keeps on going. Shouldn't everything stop?

There are not enough tears in the world to wash away the pain you feel when you see that shiny wooden coffin at the front of the church, and then see it by the mound of earth out at the windy cemetery.

Six months later Uncle Bill came to visit from Peace River. "How are you doing, Mary?" he asked. We were outside in the yard. I watched two ravens fly spirals across the golden face of the midnight sun. "I'm mad at Elizabeth Ann," I said. "I'm mad, even though she's dead and — how stupid is that to be mad at a dead person?"

Uncle Bill said, "Sounds pretty normal to me. You loved her." I was surprised. And relieved that he didn't think I was a horrible person. "Pretty normal," he said again. After that we sat together not saying anything, just watching the ravens dip and dive, swoop and soar through the wide northern sky. I loved my uncle a lot in that moment.

About a year later we learned about Fetal Alcohol Effect and Fetal Alcohol Syndrome. Shanti is the one who went after the information first. There wasn't much, but we learned that if a woman is pregnant and drinks alcohol, she can cause brain damage, actually make holes in the baby's brain. It means that part of the brain works but other parts are damaged, like the parts that control impulses, anger and healthy decision-making. Jessy is at university in Edmonton now. His big project is writing a report about how families deal with Fetal Alcoholism and how kids who have it can cope. One by one, each of us is finding a way to make meaning of Elizabeth Ann's life.

And now, when we come home to Yellowknife for Christmas holidays, we have a new tradition. On the longest night of the year, we step into the circle of light in the yard. If we are lucky, the northern lights dance across the sky. One by one, we fling ourselves into the snow and start. Keeping our heads still, we move our arms up and down, up and down to make the wings. And because she's a girl angel, we move our legs back and forth to make a skirt. Then, ever so carefully, we pull ourselves up, take three steps forward and turn. "There, Elizabeth Ann," we say, "now people can see you."

The Canoe

LEE MARACLE

. . .

Our house stands near the edge of a small salt-water lagoon about a thousand metres from the ocean on the west coast of Vancouver Island. Enclosed by the land when the tide is out, and open to the sea when it is in, the lagoon stretches out from behind a row of cedar trees bent from the wind. The trees almost block my view of the sea but not entirely, and the soft swish of the steady surf soothes, stills my thoughts. The gulls screech to one another from the shell-draped sandy edges of the lagoon, and off in the distance seals play in the water near the western edge of the land. A family of swans lives in the lagoon for part of the year. The young one ought to be learning to fly soon, but the parents don't seem too concerned or anxious about it. The sun overhead is shining, lighting the tips of the surf diamond bright as they roll forward. There are a few fluffy clouds in the sky, not enough to threaten rain. The wind coming off the sea cools the skin; it is soft and comforting. I could use a little comfort.

Our house isn't like the ones in town. It is a five-room cabin with a simple living room, dining room and big kitchen with two small bedrooms and a bathroom near the back exit. There is no basement, just a crawl space. Out here under the onslaught of salt-sea winds and rain our car has to be parked in the garage so it doesn't get salt damaged. Unlike some town folks we don't use the garage for storage. All the stuff we don't use anymore is stored in a shed. In the front of the house facing the sea is a porch as long as the house is wide. My dad built it for my mom. There is a swing on it, a two-seater. Dad built that too. I'm in it. Dad never is anymore. They used to swing on it before she died a year ago. They spent their summer evenings rocking back and forth in it, Mom knitting, and Dad reading the band mail out loud to her. That's my dad: builds a romantic swing for the love of his life and all he ever did was read band mail. From the porch I look out onto the water and wish I wasn't wound up so tight.

My dad is in the old shed. I can hear him rummaging around. I imagine him shifting things about, maybe ordering things up, and cleaning it out because he wants to start a new project. Not likely, I tell myself. He hasn't started a new project since I was ten years old. Every now and then the sound of planks hitting the sod floor with a thud reaches me and I wonder what the heck he is doing in there. To find out I would have to go there and see, but I hesitate. Another thud followed by a curse. I get halfway up, but something has my feet nailed to the floor of the porch and so I sit back down and rock the swing.

Lately things haven't been going so well between us. A quiet — strange and cumbersome — has us both trapped. It's not an easy quiet. It feels thick, damp, like some invisible and porous object separating us. The quiet is physical, powerful and at the same time fragile, like some moment could pop it. But neither of us knows how to conjure the moment, so we sidestep each other, barely looking at one another as we pass by. Every morning I get up and promise myself: today I am going to look him straight in the eye and say something. But what, I can't figure out yet. I know the quiet that traps us is because of Mom. I want to say something profound that will break the silence, but when I think of her, only little things come up, like missing the soft swish-swish of her skirt as she moved about the house. I can't just up and tell him that. I miss her smile when I caught her studying me. It seems meager to say that I would give anything to wake up and hear the quiet rattle coming from the kitchen as she cooks.

Her movements were deliberate and austere, thrifty even.

Sometimes she paused, leaned away from the cupboard, lifted her index finger to her cheek, her eyes studying the seasonings above her as she decided what she needed to brighten the meal she had planned for us. Her absence is huge, but when I try to name it, it comes out all small and petty because I miss those small moments — the way she cupped her cheek and leaned into listening to me, and the pause, the pregnancy of it, before she spoke and turned what I said into something more. If I say stuff like that to Dad it would make her death feel frail, wispy and trivial.

Another loud bang comes from the shed. My dad hollers and I jump up, but my feet won't move. He must be hurt. Something heavy must have fallen on him, and then I hear the sound of glass shattering and he lets go a delicious string of urgent-sounding curses. I bolt for the shed. By the time I get to the entrance he is lurching through the door towing the old canoe that sat up on the rafters of the shed for longer than I have been alive. There doesn't appear to be anything wrong with him, but the canoe looks like it could use a little tender loving care. Apparently on its way down the canoe fell through an old window, but the flying glass missed Dad.

"Hey," he pumps it out like he has done something he is proud of and I ought to commend him. My teeth grind a little. I'm trying not to be too mad about the false alarm and I fight the embarrassment of over-reacting to his cussing.

"Hey what?" the sarcasm in my voice is born of a year of resentment. Dad ignores it. He keeps smiling. He hasn't smiled for awhile. He looks good for a change. Geez, I think, don't throw water on his fire; it isn't going to help. Can't I just this once let him think I am happy about whatever he is proud of? "Geez!" And I realize that like a dummy I just said that out loud. It is out there and I can't take it back, so I do the Indian thing, just pretend I didn't say anything. He does too.

"I thought we'd have a look at this old tub. See if she still floats, if she does, maybe we can take a ride?" I swallow and think, what if it leaks? It is one more thing you can be disappointed about, Dad, one more reason to drift deeper into silence. I let out the air I was holding in my lungs with a loud sigh, a sigh of relief.

He ignores my sigh. "Give me a hand, boy?"

The canoe was built by Dad's granddad. It is so old the cedar is a pale gray on the ridges of the wood grain, while the valleys are dark, near black. Great Grandpa carved it during the cultural prohibition days, so he did his best to make it look like a giant skiff with no paint and no Indian designs on it like you see on canoes these days. As a skiff, our dugout is plain ugly. Even so, Mom had dreamed that we might restore it. But it doesn't sound like a great idea to test it while the surf is up. Still, I can't bring myself to be the reason for Dad's disappointment, so I swing around to the other side and drop back a little distance and pick up the canoe.

We raise her up to our thighs and we head to sea trying not to scrape the bottom on the rocks that dot the land before the sandy edge of shoreline. The tide is part way out and the mudflats are covered in seaweed and kelp. This makes the walk to the sea comic. We teeter and totter forward, nearly dropping the canoe with every step. I look around to see if anyone is watching. Thank god everyone went to town. Pop hasn't done this for awhile and I have never done this before, so we are not as steady on our feet as we need to be, but neither of us seems to be able to stop. We stagger, slip, slide, recover our balance and stagger some more toward the open water. With every slip-slide I convince myself that this is the dumbest thing we have ever decided to do, to test out a hundred-year-old shabby half-skiff-shaped canoe with a six-foot surf up. But I keep putting one foot in front of the other as if my brain has just up and gone.

"We really should pitch it first, but there isn't any sense doing that unless we know she is seaworthy, right?" He wants me to agree, so I do, smiling stupidly. He looks so damn happy, it is contagious. My knees quiver with fear, but I smile because part of me is having a blast. I can't stop thinking about how truly dumb this is, dangerous even, but at the same time there is a butterfly of joy bubbling around in my belly and I can't stop hauling this tub to the sea. There is no one around to make sure we get back to shore if it isn't seaworthy. Even with his back turned, Dad looks warm, as if the damp, quiet cylinder he was trapped in has evaporated. This is the first time I have felt this good doing something with my dad, and even if it is the dumbest thing to do, I am doing it.

Things weren't all that great between us even when Mom was alive. Now that she is dead, there doesn't seem any way to heal the rift. He always talked about me to her, even when I was right there in front of him, "Your son needs to learn to fish" or "Your son needs to learn to mow the lawn." Then she negotiated with me that it was time to learn and she sent me out with the "wall of silence" that he was. From the day I learned something new it became a personal chore. Sometimes he was there with me, raking while I mowed or gutting fish I caught, but we never were truly together. I was her son, not his. Mom tried to bridge the distance between us to soften the space, but she was never successful.

Dad has been moping silently since she died. He looks old and lost without her, like she made everything, even me seem worth his while. So a few months after Mom died, when my cousin Joey suggested going down to the S-turns where all the kids on the rez go to drink, I jumped at the chance. I wanted to blind myself from seeing Mom. It seemed a better idea than rattling off some list of things I missed and ruining my memory of her.

He caught me. I was drunk as a skunk when I heard the old pickup pull up and saw him jump out and head for me, lips pulled so tight I couldn't see them and he has very big square Indian lips. He hollered so loud I half sobered up.

He grabbed me by the scruff of the neck and dragged me to the pickup. He threw me in the back so hard I scraped my elbow and tore my jacket. The old truck kicked up a cloud of dust as he sped away from the turns. He drove so fast I bounced around in the back thinking any minute I would fly out of the truck. I grabbed the rings on the toolbox bolted to the floor and hung on so tight my skin burned. When he pulled up to the house he slammed on the brakes. I flew forward and hit my head on the front of the pickup box.

Mercilessly, he strode around to the back and dragged me out of the pickup by the feet paying no attention to my bleeding head. He shoved me several times toward the front door. I staggered and fought to keep upright. He didn't say a word. The longer his quiet lasted, the more scared I became. Inside he poured a tall glass of water and added several tablespoons of salt. I wanted to cry for Mom. I wanted to sink into a chair, put my head in my hands and weep. I prayed for my dead grandma to come get me. I prayed for my mom to come and get me, for the floor to swallow me, even for lightning to strike me, but no one came except Dad and nothing happened. There was only the glass of salt water standing between us.

He handed it to me and ordered me to drink. I drank. I vomited. He ordered me to drink more. I threw up half the night. I heard him say, "Have another drink, you fool." I did, and then I vomited some more.

The next day he kicked the end of my bed and shouted, "Get up." I scrambled into my jeans, tossed my shirt on and jumped into my sneakers. This shameful feeling of wanting to do anything to please him swept through me, just so he would calm down and stop being so angry.

"Get in the truck." The look on his face scared me more now that I was sober. He was madder than I had ever seen him. My dad has always been a crusty man with a short fuse, but I got used to that early. The crustiness had never been this furious. My legs were shaking so hard I could hardly walk. I fought the urge to wet my pants. His eyes stayed cold and furious as he drove the pickup across the reserve.

He stopped at the S-turns and my heart sank. What is he going to do to me? He handed me a garbage bag. Through his teeth he growled, "Clean it up." Clean it up? At first I was relieved, but then I took a look around. The S-turns were an incredible mess, years of teenage party filth and memorabilia lay everywhere. Garbage is repulsive. I really didn't want to do this. I did not make this mess by myself. Some of the garbage was so old I pictured my dad creating it. It wasn't fair. I looked up to say something and saw his face. It was hateful. I dared not argue with him.

Dad sat in the truck while I picked up every old paper wrapping, pop bottle, beer bottle and cigarette butt until the bag was full. I tossed the bag into the truck and then I saw his arm reach out the window. In his hand was another bag. The sun beat down on me, the sweat poured out of me, and I endured my first hangover, picking up the dirtiest bunch of garbage imaginable and wondering if I was going to make it to manhood. After awhile, I succumbed to the work at hand. I challenged myself to be thorough, to be quick and careful.

After I filled four bags, I stood beside the box of the pick-up waiting for whatever was to come next. Dad signaled me to get in beside him. I did not want to get in next to all that hate and rage but I got in. I sat up as straight as I could. If I didn't feel brave, at least I could look the part. Dad looked out the window on his side. He stared out the window without starting the truck for a few seconds.

"Son, I'm no good at this parenting stuff. Your momma always took care of that. She . . ." His voice cracked. I fought back a sob I dared not let go because underneath it were more sobs, big wracking ones.

"I am damned sure that she didn't want you hanging out drunk by the S-turns. She wanted better things for you." He leaned onto the steering wheel, then his head dropped onto his arms and he moved his head from side to side like a half-blind big old bear trying to see something.

"I'll try to get better at parenting, but you have to find the strength in yourself never to violate her memory." He sat up, put the keys into the ignition, turned the engine over and slowly drove home.

That was a month ago. Since then he just walks sad and

silent. That doesn't feel much better than his rage but it does fuel my desire to please a little. I definitely did not want to join Joey and the others by the S-turns, not so much for fear of Dad, but out of respect for Mom. He was right, she wanted more for me, and even if I don't feel like I want more for myself right now I should at least fake it until I do.

I was beginning to feel all right when Pop got the idea to drag out the old canoe. And so I let myself be talked into his lame-brained plan. Okay, Pop, I tell myself, there is a six-foot surf out there and very likely this old canoe will capsize. We may sink out there, but we can both swim and hopefully we will capsize while we are still in shallow water. So let's do it. If we don't try, my guilt will choke the life out of me anyway.

Out close to the water is the tide line. It is slippery, full of seaweed, kelp and bits of dead wood and other debris. Suddenly Dad's leg goes straight out and he topples. On the way down he drops his side of the canoe and it lands on a rock in the middle of the tide line. The canoe cracks. Doggone it. I volley between feeling lucky and feeling destined to live a life of guilt.

I put my side down carefully, though this is as stupid as trying to launch the boat, since the canoe is already busted and care would not do any good now. Dad is still lying in the mud. I offer my hand. I am still scared, so my hand is quivering. He looks at it, grabs it and pulls me down instead of helping himself up. As I slop about in the mud beside him he pops a guffaw that leads him straight to hysterical laughter. It is contagious. I laugh too. We both laugh till we cry.

Once the crying came it grew into the biggest crying I ever experienced. We leaned on the broken canoe and cried over Mom's dream of reviving this old boat, we cried over not being a good dad or a good son, and finally we knew we were both crying over what we had lost. We stopped only when we were too exhausted to shed another tear.

The incoming tide tickled our feet by the time we finished. I looked up at the sun shining down on us and it dawned on me that I knew how to be a son to my mother, but I did not know how to be a son to my father. I don't want to say anything bad about my mom. She was the most loving being in our lives, but she didn't do us any favours by fixing things between us. We never learned to get along without her. We have been around each other for fifteen years and yet neither of us has a clue how to enjoy being together. I leaned my head into my dad's shoulder.

"Remember you said you don't know how to parent a son?"

Dad flinched, then let go a cautious "Yeah" like he didn't really want to have to pay for his honesty, his helplessness or his rage, but like a champ he stepped up to the plate to take his medicine. "Well, I really don't know how to be your son either. Mom's gone, so I can't be her son anymore. I have to learn to be yours."

"We're in a helluva fix then, aren't we?" And we laughed again. He jumped up and headed for the house. I wasn't sure that the conversation was over so I just stood there looking at his receding back. The water sneaked up and curled around my wet shoes before he turned.

"Well, first thing you have to know about being my son is that I don't stand around waiting for someone to tell us what to do, and you shouldn't either. The boat is busted and the tide is up, so that idea is over. We will learn to be father and son in the coming years as one thing leads us to the next." I followed him up to the house.

"What's next?"

"Supper," he dropped flatly.

On the porch, he peeled off his wet clothes and I did too. I could see the youthful swan trying to fly and nodded in its direction. Dad and I stood half-naked, dripping wet and watched that swan take flight. The swan lacked elegance and strength at first. In near full flight he weakened, then came crashing down toward the sea. His wings nearly disappeared into the surf. I tensed. I felt like that swan, graceless and not quite strong enough for manhood. "Fly boy, fly," I whispered and by some miracle the swan found the will and grace to flap his wings and raise himself up again. I watched, relieved.

"Supper sounds good," I said, and breaking off a cedar branch, gently tossed it in the direction of the swan. I thanked the swan, my dad and my mom. Dad was holding the door open. As I entered he touched my shoulder just barely. There was a new sweetness in the lightness of his touch. Inside he pulled the last quart of fish my mom had canned last year from the shelf and handed me a paring knife.

"You peel the potatoes and I'll make salmon patties." We puttered about the kitchen in silence for awhile. I couldn't help chuckling quietly to myself about the picture we must have made as we rolled about in the mud. One chuckle reached the air and I looked over to Pop whose eyes smiled brightly.

"We can make another," he said stirring the patties he was frying.

"Canoe? You know how to do that?" I asked surprised.

"Nah, but it can't be that hard, an adze, a log and some fire is all we need." I just stared at him. Is he nuts? No, he must be joking.

"Well, someone must have dreamed that first canoe into being." He was serious. Momma had dreams. Dad hadn't much cared to dream with her when she was alive, but now he was picking up her bundle. I choked a little as I realized her dreams must have centred on me. My dad was determined to realize them for her, one step at a time.

All is Calm

ANN WALSH

. . .

I was the only one who could do it, and it was turning out to be worse than I thought it would be. I mean, I love my Grandma: everyone loves their grandmother, right? But my Gran had become, well, strange isn't quite the word. Mom said it was Alzheimer's and she cried when she told me. It didn't mean much to me at the time, but as the year went by I learned more than I ever wanted to know about that disease.

It makes people forget. Not ordinary forgetting — the square roots of numbers or your last boyfriend's phone number — but serious blanking out, like the names of your friends, what you do in a bathroom, and whether your bra goes on before or after you put on your blouse. My Gran hadn't forgotten those things yet, but chances were she *would* as the disease took her further and further away from the person she once had been. She still had good days, times when she seemed so normal, so like her old self that it made it worse when she went off into whatever strange place the Alzheimer's was taking her mind. She had always been a bit "odd" — actually "ditsy" was the word my father used — but she had been kind and funny and caring and clean. But now, sometimes, she was really different, weird even, and here I was on a bus with her at four o'clock on a Wednesday afternoon hoping that today would be one of her good days.

I was the only one who could do it, take Gran to the doctor's appointment. Mom was away at a conference, my brother had to get his braces adjusted, and Dad couldn't get off work in time.

"I'm sorry, Katie," Mom said before she left for her conference, " I know you don't want to take her; she can be difficult. But she *has* to go. It took us months to get the appointment. This specialist can help us get Gran into a care facility — he has to classify her condition as serious so that we can put her in a place where she'll be looked after properly. I can't do it anymore. She's only lived with us a year, but I can't handle her anymore."

Mom looked as if she were going to cry again when she said that. She'd been doing a lot of crying lately.

I knew I had to do it, but I didn't want to. Going anywhere with Gran lately was an adventure, and not the good kind of adventure. You never knew how — or sometimes *who* she was going to be. Each day, each minute was different. I only hoped that there wouldn't be many people on the bus with us, especially no one I knew.

Maybe the day of her doctor's appointment would be one of Gran's good days, I thought. Maybe everything would be fine.

"It's all right, Mom," I said putting my arm around her, saying all the right things about how I didn't mind at all, and sure, it was only a short bus trip, and no, Gran would be fine and so would I. "Don't worry," I reassured her. "I'll manage."

I was managing. Barely.

It started when I got home from school the day of the doctor's appointment. Mom had left a note, reminding Gran to be ready by half-past three, and Dad had phoned her at noon reminding her again, but she hadn't picked up the phone. I heard his anxious voice when I checked the answering machine. At three-thirty, an hour before we had to be at the doctor's, Gran was sitting at the kitchen table in her nightgown writing Christmas cards. At least she *thought* she was writing them. She'd found a box of new cards in a drawer where Mom had stored them, and she'd written the same address on every envelope — no name, just the address of the house she used to live in. She was singing to herself when I got home, singing Christmas carols and stuffing blank cards into envelopes — in March.

It took a while, but I got her dressed and we got out of the house and down to the bus stop in record time. The bus came along right away, and I thought that everything might be okay. I was proud of myself; I'd managed to get Gran this far and it wasn't a long bus trip. "Hey, Mom," I thought. "See? I told you I could manage."

Then Gran started singing again. "Silent night, holy night, all is calm . . ." She has a loud voice, loud and friendly, the kind of voice you wanted to hear singing happy birthday to you when you were nine, but on a crowded bus it didn't sound friendly. It sounded weird.

I said "Gran, it's not Christmas. Don't sing that song now."

Behind me, I heard someone laugh. I turned around to see who it was, but no one was looking at me. They were all busy staring out the windows or concentrating on the ads on the walls.

Except for one person, sitting near the back of the bus. He waved cheerily at me. "Hi, Katie."

I whirled around, pretending I hadn't seen him.

It was Kevin. Why did he, of all people, have to be on this bus? He was on the school council and captain of the soccer team. He had deep blue eyes with crinkles around the edges when he smiled. And Kevin smiled a lot, because to him everything was funny — he was always joking, even managing to make some of the teachers laugh during class.

He belonged to a group of kids just like him, except the girls were cheerleaders, not jocks. They ate together at "their" table in the cafeteria and hung out in a bunch between classes and after school. I was surprised Kevin even knew my name. He'd never spoken to me before, although we were in a couple of the same classes this semester.

I didn't wave back, just shrank down in the seat. Maybe he'd think he was wrong, that it was someone else, not me, sitting beside the crazy singing woman. Otherwise I knew he'd tell his friends about seeing me and Gran. I could hear them whispering the next time I walked past them in the hall. I could hear them humming "Silent night . . ." I could hear their laughter.

"Don't sing now, Gran," I said again. "Please, stop."

She did. But she stared at me with her mouth open, as if it had frozen on the phrase "mother and child."

"Katherine?" she said in a small voice. Then her face crumpled and she began to cry.

Out loud. Cry as if I had kicked her, or told her that her puppy had been run over. "Don't cry, Gran," I said quickly. "Listen, you can sing all you want to once we get home."

She clutched at my hand, and suddenly the tears were gone. "That will be fun," she said. "Can we go carol singing? I'll make hot chocolate and we'll go out in the snow and sing."

"Sure, Gran," I said, trying to untangle my hand. "Sure, when Christmas comes we'll go carol singing."

She smiled at me, and I gave up trying to get my hand away from hers, just held it. Gran has a nice smile. She looks at you when she smiles, looks right in your eyes, and you know that smile is for you and not for anyone else.

She was quiet for three stops, then suddenly she shouted, "Where are we going?"

I jumped. So did almost everyone else on the bus. I could see the driver squinting at his rear-view mirror, trying to see who was making all the noise.

"Shhh. It's all right, Gran," I said, squeezing her hand, hoping she'd settle down. She didn't.

She yanked her hand away from mine. "Why are we going this way?" she demanded loudly. "We'll get lost." Again I thought I heard someone behind me laughing. This time I didn't turn around to see who it was. Although I hadn't recognized the voice, I was sure it was Kevin.

Heads were turning as the people in front of us took quick looks at my — at the crazy old lady who used to be my Grandma. I tried not to meet anyone's eyes. "We won't get lost, Gran," I reassured, patting her arm. "This is the way to the doctor's office. I know where we're going. It's all right."

I spoke softly, hoping she'd get the idea and lower her voice, too. It didn't make any difference. "Stop the bus, stop it. We're lost!" This time she yelled the words even more loudly than before.

Once more there was laughter from behind me. I tried to ignore it.

"We have to get off. Right now." Gran stood up awkwardly. Then the bus lurched away from a stop and she fell backwards into her seat.

"It's all right, Gran. Everything's going to be all right," I said, my voice trembling. "Please, believe me. We're not lost."

And then, like the sun coming out from behind a cloud, she smiled at me and, as if everything was normal and fine she said, "Isn't it a lovely day, Katherine? It's so nice to spend some time with you, dear. Shall we have tea after our appointment? You always like those sticky buns they make at the Tea Shoppe."

She had come back. Just like that. One moment there was this crazy person sitting beside me, and the next moment my grandmother was back. Suddenly I felt like crying, too.

I reached out and took her hand again, held it tightly. She didn't say another word for the rest of the trip.

Then it was our stop. I stood up. "Come on, Gran," I said. "We're here."

Her face changed again. She grabbed onto the back of the seat in front of her and said, "I'm not moving. You're trying to trick me."

"Gran," I urged, hoping that this time she hadn't gone too far away into the craziness of the disease, "Gran, come on." I took her arm and tried gently to pull her to her feet, but she clutched the handrail tighter.

"Leave me alone," she said, her voice loud and harsh. "I don't know you. I don't go anywhere with strangers."

"You do know me, Gran. I'm Katie. Katherine. I'm taking you to see the doctor, remember? This is where his office is."

"Leave me alone," she said again. "Don't touch me. Please, someone help me!" I couldn't believe it. She was calling for help as if I were trying to kidnap her.

"Gran," I said desperately, "please, we have to get off here."

"Everything all right back there?" called the driver, turning around and halfway rising from his seat. "I've got a schedule to keep, miss. You'll have to get her off the bus quickly. I can't wait any longer."

"I'm never going anywhere with *you*," Gran said to me. "I hate you. You're a nasty little girl." The doors of the bus closed and the driver pulled slowly ahead. I stood in the aisle, wondering what on earth I could do. One thing I knew I mustn't do, though, was get angry. It wasn't my Gran talking. It was the disease, the Alzheimer's. I had to remember that. Mom had told us over and over that Gran didn't mean to be cruel or to say mean things, but the disease took over her voice as it took over her mind. She couldn't control the words that came out of her mouth.

It's the disease speaking, I told myself firmly, only the disease, not my Gran. Fine. But the stupid disease wasn't going to let her get off the bus and what could I do about it? I sat down beside her again and put my arm around her shoulders. "Please, Gran, try to remember. It's me, Katie."

The bus began to slow, approaching the next stop. I didn't hear Kevin come up behind me, but suddenly he was there. "Good afternoon, ma'am," he said, looking down at my grandmother. "Can I help you?"

"It's okay," I said stiffly. "We'll manage."

"Really? Looks as if you could use some help."

"Not from you. You think she's funny."

"That's not true, Katie."

"I can manage," I said again. "Leave us alone."

But Gran was smiling up at Kevin, smiling her wonderful warm smile. "What a nice young man," she said. "Yes, please help me. I'm lost."

I didn't want Kevin's help. But I was desperate. If he thought he could get her off the bus, I'd let him try. Even though I knew he was just doing it to collect material for his new stand-up comic act called "When I Saw Katie on the Bus." Opening in a cafeteria near you tomorrow at lunch. Don't miss it. It's a million laughs.

What else could I do? I stood up and moved out of the way.

Kevin offered Gran his arm. She took it and he ushered her out of her seat, then down the stairwell. He went ahead of her out of the doors, then turned back and held out his arm again as she stepped down. "Thank you," she said, smiling at him. "Thank you so much. You've been very helpful."

"No problem, ma'am," he said. "I think your doctor's office is one block back. Would you like me to walk there with you and Katie?"

"Katie?" said Gran, puzzled. Then she saw me and the glazed look left her eyes. She, my Gran, was back again. "Katie, hurry up," she said. "We don't want to be late for our appointment, do we? Afterwards we'll have tea. Perhaps your young man would like to join us?" She slung her handbag over her shoulder, straightened the scarf around the neck of her coat and strode off, heading in the right direction, walking tall and proud.

I followed her. Kevin followed me. I turned around and glared at him. "Goodbye, Kevin," I said. "Thanks. I guess. But you should be thanking *me*. You got a good laugh out of her."

"Laugh? I wasn't laughing."

"I heard you."

He looked hurt. "That wasn't me. It was some jerk sitting behind me. I don't think he was right in the head — he was talking to himself when he got off at the last stop."

"Come on. It was you."

"No, Katie, it wasn't. Believe me, I don't think your grandmother is funny."

"It wasn't you?" I said, surprised. "But I thought . . ."

"You thought wrong," he said abruptly.

"Sorry," I said. "I mean, thank you for the help." Then the tears that I'd been fighting for almost the whole trip won the battle and I began to bawl. I didn't want to cry, not here, not at all, but I couldn't stop the tears. Kevin awkwardly patted my arm.

"It's okay, go ahead and cry as much as you need to. I'll keep an eye on her."

He gestured to my grandmother, who had stopped in front of a grocery store and was staring at a crate of oranges as if she had never seen fruit before. Well, maybe she hadn't.

In the world she lived in these days, perhaps there weren't any oranges. Or any apples or bananas or granddaughters.

After a minute I blew my nose. "I'm okay now," I said and it was almost true. "I've got to get her to her doctor's appointment. Thanks again. You were great with her. I don't know what I would have done if you hadn't helped get her off the bus."

Then it struck me. Here was this guy I barely knew — why did he help me with my ditsy grandmother? Why did he care?

It was almost as if Kevin read my thoughts. He grinned at me. "Yeah," he said. "Didn't you know that your grandma is my type?"

I tried to grin back. "I didn't know that. But I guess I don't know you well enough to know what your type is, do I?"

"We'll work on that," he said. "I think we've a lot in common, more than you realize."

"A lot in common . . . ?" I began, puzzled. Then I saw him looking down the street at my Gran and I remembered how patient he'd been with her and I thought I understood.

"Your grandmother, too?" I asked. "Your grandmother has Alzheimer's?"

"Not my grandmother. Not even my grandfather. It's my father. The doctors call it 'early onset' which means it starts when someone's younger. Dad's only forty-six."

"I didn't know younger people could get Alzheimer's," I said, surprised.

"It happens sometimes. Not very often."

If it was this hard for me and my family with Gran, how much harder would it be for Kevin and his family? At forty-six people weren't supposed to be ditsy. They were supposed to be holding down jobs, helping with homework and cheering for their kid's soccer team.

"Oh, Kevin," I said. "I'm sorry."

And I was. Sorry for Kevin and what he had to go through as his father went away to that special hell where people with Alzheimer's live; sorry for my family and me for what we had to go through with Gran; sorry for the embarrassment and pain and ugliness that was ahead and couldn't be avoided. I was sorry for all of us, but I knew we'd get through it, we'd survive.

But my Gran and Kevin's father, they wouldn't get through it. They *wouldn't* survive except as lonely shadows of themselves in a world where nothing makes sense and no one was familiar.

I went up to my Gran who was still staring at the oranges, and right there in the middle of the sidewalk with people all around us, I hugged her. "I love you, Gran," I said. "I'll always love you."

She looked me right in the eyes and smiled that warm, wonderful smile of hers. Then, from somewhere far, far away she said, "I love you too, Mary."

A version of "All Is Calm" first appeared in *The Blue Jean Collection* edited by Peter Carver (Thistledown Press, 1992).

Kick

BETTY JANE HEGERAT

. . .

Justin decides even before he leaves the school at lunchtime that he's not going to tell his mom about Will. She'll find out soon enough. In the parking lot he spies a rock with a good edge. About the size of a haki sack. A sweet kick sends the stone flying down the street with Justin panting after it. He can hear Amanda calling behind him but he ignores her.

When he opens the front door, he can smell fish and green onion.

In the kitchen, his mom, still in her housecoat, shuffles from the fridge to the counter, mixing tuna for sandwiches.

"Stinks in here," he says, and when she yawns, he asks, "Did you sleep?" She worked twelve-hour shifts all weekend and now has four days off. When Justin left for school she was trying to decide whether to sleep or tough it out.

"Some," she says. She whacks a sandwich into quarters, and slides the plate in front of him. "Remember this when I'm old. Any mom who got up out of her bed after three hours of sleep to make lunch for a fourteen-year-old deserves big boxes of chocolates in The Home."

Justin opens a sandwich and picks out the onion. His mom rolls her eyes, but waits until he's finished before she scoops up the pile of green and drops it down the garburetor. Then she scrubs her hands under the tap as if she's at work. She's a nurse, and Justin's sure their kitchen is clean enough for brain surgery. He makes a tower of the four pieces of sandwich.

She pours a glass of milk, sets it in front of him. Musses his hair, and then wrinkles her nose. "You didn't shower this morning."

"Sure I did," he lies. He presses hard on the sandwiches, flattening the bread the way he likes it. But the first bite makes him gag. The same feeling in the back of his throat as this morning when Mr. Waters stood in front of homeroom blinking so fast it looked as if there were insects behind the lenses of his glasses. "Class, we have terrible news today."

Justin coughs the wad of sandwich into a napkin.

His mom watches his face for a minute and then puts her hand on his forehead. "What's up?"

"My throat feels funny." He glugs down half of the milk.

"That's all I want." Swiping away the milk mustache with the back of his hand, he stands up. When she has that squinty look, she can read his mind. "I better go."

Still squinting. "Did something happen this morning?"

Oh yeah. Something happened all right. He mumbles and stumbles through the stuff Mr. Waters told them. About Will and his mom and dad and his sisters in the van in California. And somebody came through that red light and Will's dad couldn't stop.

"Oh my God, Justin!" She grabs him and pulls him so close he can feel her heart thumping like it's his own. His face is pressed to the night-time smell of her housecoat. "How terrible for Will and his family! Are they okay? Was anyone else hurt?"

She's got it wrong, but he can't correct her. He just shakes his head and pulls away. With the tips of her fingers between her lips she looks like a little kid. He knows that as soon as he leaves the house, she'll flop down in the rocker in the living room and stare at the wall. He wishes he wasn't going to walk out the door and leave her thinking Will's dad is dead. But she'll have a worse afternoon if she knows it's Will.

Halfway to school, still booting the rock, the inside of his foot starts to ache. A soft mushy hurt like pressing on an old bruise. A glance at his watch and he slows down so that he can time his arrival to the bell. There are clumps of grade eights standing around the door. Girls crying and holding each other the way they did this morning. Except for Amanda who swoops down on him at the edge of the parking lot. She hooks her foot in front of his and lofts his rock onto the playing field.

"Why didn't you wait for me, you dork? I was calling you."

She's about four inches taller than he is this year. His mom says the boys will catch up in high school, that Justin will grow into his weight. But for now he still feels like a blimp, which is why he goes home for lunch. He doesn't need anyone ragging him about stuffing his face.

Amanda says she goes home because the girls in grade eight are morons and she doesn't want to hang out with them. She says she can't wait to go back up north for the summer. Jason and Amanda have been friends since kindergarten. She and her mom live across the street with Amanda's grandparents. Every summer Amanda spends a month in Yellowknife with her dad and her other grandmother. At the end of August, she comes back acting like some kind of junior shaman with a new supply of bones and feathers and other stuff her mom won't let her keep in their house. Most of it is in a box under Justin's bed.

They wait on the fringe. "Sucks, huh?" she says. She's chewing on her thumbnail, looking away from Justin whenever he glances toward her. "Will's such a turd, but I never hoped he'd die."

Justin feels like she kicked him in the gut. Maybe she

never hoped Will would die, but she has to know that Justin did. Every time Will yanked the toque off Justin's head and filled it with snow, snatched his backpack and threw it in the air and all his pencils and homework tumbled into the wind. Every time Will puffed out his cheeks and grinned and said, "Justin's got high cholesterol!" Every single time, he wished Will would drop dead. But there was always Amanda, helping him brush the snow off his stuff, stomping along beside him all the way home, shouting at him. "Justin, you have to be a bear! Nobody messes with Bear!"

Finally the bell rings, and they trail in together. They have math with Mr. Waters first period after lunch, so back to their home room.

Justin slides into his desk and looks straight ahead, over top of the empty chair in front of him. Are they going to leave it there? Waters hands out a letter for parents. He says it's about the memorial service for Will. The math test on Thursday is postponed because he knows that some of the students will want to attend.

Justin folds the letter and crams it into his pocket. Mr. Waters is still talking. "For those of you who were friends of Will, there's a counsellor in the office this afternoon." He begins to point and call out names. And the first one out of his mouth is "Justin."

Friends? Does Waters think he's doing Justin a favour by including him? Amanda says thanks but no thanks when he calls her name. "I really didn't know him very well," she says. Justin wishes he'd thought of that line, but more than anything he wants to get out of the room, so he shuffles to the door with everyone else.

In the hall, he waits until they're ahead of him, the girls whispering and sniffing, and then ducks into the washroom. Sits there on a toilet and watches the minutes click past on his wrist. He knows the routine with the counsellor. When his grade five teacher's baby died, a counsellor came to the classroom. To help them "make sense of it" the principal said. Like there's any sense in babies dying. Justin already knew from his mom's job at the hospital that shitty things happen to kids.

After half an hour, he peeks down the hall. Through the glass wall in the office, he can see a few of his classmates waiting in the chairs. Girls. The ones who probably never even talked to Will.

Finally, Justin slips back into the classroom, into his desk. Amanda is looking at him out of the corner of her eye.

He closes his eyes and tries to drown out the voices. Since morning, he's been afraid to think about Will. Afraid he'll see him all mangled and bloody. But instead, he's imagining Will in the chair in front of him. Will turning with that twisted grin, lifting a cheek, and polluting the air around Justin. Then holding his nose, and just loud enough for everyone to hear, "Ewwwww. Justin! Silent but deadly!"

Justin gags. He swears he can smell the fart even though it's a dream. He gets up without telling Mr. Waters where he's going and runs for the washroom. After he spits into the sink, he rinses his mouth, and then hides in a cubicle until the bell rings for the next class.

At dismissal, the haki sack guys hang out in the stairwell. Sometimes Justin spies on them from the top of the stairs after everyone else is gone. Pretends to be waiting for someone. Usually they're playing "clock" and he fingers the knitted grey footbag in his pocket, knowing that he's better than any of them. A guy like Will — if he did normal stuff like haki instead of following Justin around — would kick in and join them, all jokey. But Justin's not good at jokey, and he doesn't need anyone telling him to get lost. Today, he races ahead, wanting to be first out of the school.

The rock is in the soccer field one bounce from a Slurpee cup, exactly where he marked it in his mind. Kick, kick, kick, takes him halfway home before Amanda catches up.

"So what did she tell you?"

Justin shrugs. Lines up the rock with his toe, and wraps his fingers around the haki in his pocket. The dense weave has a comfortable scratchy feel.

"You didn't go, did you? I'll bet you sat in the can the whole time." After the kick, she races beside him. Amanda is the only person he knows who can talk in a normal voice when she's running full-out. "So are you going to the funeral?"

He stops, and bends over to catch his breath. "Are you?"

"I dunno," she says. "Maybe. If you go." Then Amanda

turns and races ahead of him. From behind, it looks as though she's flying, one foot hardly back on the ground before the other rises. In front of her house, she waves without looking back.

His mom meets him at the door. Hands on his shoulders, she makes him look straight into her eyes. "Why didn't you tell me it was Will who died, not his dad?"

"I did. But you misunderstood. I didn't want to talk about it, okay?"

Her hands drift down his arms, squeeze his wrists and let go. She nods. "Okay. I called the school. They said they had a counsellor talk to the class. How was that?"

He hates lying to her. Most of the time, he gets away with half the truth. "Stupid," he says. "They said it was for Will's friends, and Waters made me go."

"And . . . ?"

"I didn't even like Will!"

"Oh. Oh, I see." She has that look on her face. Like she understands everything, but she doesn't. Not any of it. She heads for the couch now, leading him by the hand. "Sit down a minute." Her eyes are shiny. She takes a Kleenex out of her pocket. There's a whole wad on the floor beside her chair. "Know why I'm crying?"

"Well yeah. A kid died. It's sad."

"All afternoon I've been imagining how I'd feel if it was you. And feeling so glad that it wasn't. Because maybe if it was someone else's boy, then that means that particular tragedy is used up and it can't happen around here again. Do you understand?"

Oh jeez, same as when they're going to fly somewhere and she says she's relieved if there's already been a plane crash in the last few months because it decreases the chances. Statistics. And then she feels guilty for being glad that other people crashed.

"Yeah," he says. He's tired, suddenly. He feels like putting his head on her shoulder. Instead, he pats her hand. And she smiles. "Guilt, right?" he asks. "You feel guilty."

"Uh huh. How about you? Do you feel guilty because you didn't like Will, and now he's dead?"

"No," Justin says. "I feel guilty, because I don't feel guilty." He's afraid for a minute that she'll think he's trying to be a smartass, but she keeps on nodding. He pulls the folded paper out of his pocket and hands it to her. His gut is rumbling. He'd like to grate some cheddar and make nachos.

She reads the letter, and looks up at him. "I think we should go to this service."

"Maybe," he says. If he says no, the discussion will go on for much longer.

She smoothes the paper on her knee and looks thoughtful. "You know, funerals are for making peace, Justin. Maybe you could go and just think about what you'd have said to Will if you'd known he was going on a trip and it would end this way."

Whoa! Glad you're leaving, but sorry you're going to die,

Jerk? Yeah, that sounds like something the counsellor lady would have suggested.

His mom is frowning, waiting for him to answer. "Justin?"

"Yeah, sure. If we go, maybe I'll do that. Think about what I'd say to him."

"So we'll go to the funeral."

"Maybe," he says. "If Amanda comes."

Amanda, all in black, looks like a raven. Black pants, black sweater, and her black hair loose on her shoulders. She barges into Justin's bedroom on Thursday afternoon while he's changing from school clothes into his khakis and button shirt. Ten seconds before, he was tugging on the pants, zipping his fly. His shirt is unbuttoned, his feet bare. "Crap, Amanda! Can't you knock?"

She shrugs and spreads out on his bed, head on the pillow, arms wide. "I don't think we should go," she says.

"Well it's too late. My mom won't back down now, and your grandma and your mom said they thought it was a good idea for you to come with us." The buttons seem too big for the holes. He works his way slowly to the bottom. When he looks up, Amanda is taking deep breaths and then exhaling as though she's going to die. "What are you doing?"

"Justin," she says in a squeaky voice that does not sound at all like Amanda, "I think I killed him."

"What?" He stares at her. "That's ridiculous. Their van got hit by another car. In California."

"I know," she whispers, "but I think I made it happen."

"Aw man!" He can't take this. Not one of Amanda's visions. Not today.

She lurches up and swings her feet to the floor. "See, I made this amulet about a month ago."

"You put a curse on Will." His voice is as heavy as the stone in his stomach. "Amanda, that's kid's stuff and you know it."

"I did not put a curse on anyone, you moron. Shamanism is about communicating, not about evil spells. I made this amulet to put you in touch with Bear. So that you would be strong and Will would never bother you again. I think it may have backfired." She swoops down beside the bed and lifts the corner of the mattress. Her hand emerges holding a cloth bag. With her teeth, she rips open the stitching at one end and tumbles the contents onto the quilt.

Will kneels beside the bed and picks through the two chicken bones, a clump of orange hair, and a tiny translucent claw. He holds it between thumb and first finger. "And this would be . . . ? The claw of the sacred grizzly?"

"Right. Symbolically. Actually it's one of Dandy's claws."

The clump of orange hair was obviously donated by Amanda's cat as well. Justin stuffs the bits back into the little bag and hands it to her. "I don't want any amulets, Amanda. I just want to get this over with."

On the way to the funeral home, Justin's mom tells them it's not really a funeral, but a memorial service. There won't be a casket. Amanda, who seems to have left her guilt in Justin's bedroom, chats with his mom about cremation versus burial. Justin refuses to have an opinion, and stares out the window, wishing he'd been a bear instead of a rabbit when his mom suggested this.

When they park at the funeral home, he considers faking a sick stomach. Like that works when your mom is a nurse. He follows Amanda in black and his mom in her navy coat and high-heeled shoes into a lobby where clumps of people stand talking quietly. He can't spot any of the other guys from school, but Mr. Waters glides over to say he's proud of Justin for coming. Even Justin's mom can't think of a comeback to that one.

Justin's already told his mom that the deal is they leave right after the service. No standing around after, no talking to Will's family. He figures the last thing Will's parents need is to see other kids today. Live kids.

On a table in front of the chapel door, there's a blown-up photo of Will in a baseball uniform. He's winding up to pitch with a look of intense concentration. Justin doesn't remember ever seeing that expression on Will's face. With the blue eyes and the blonde afro like a huge halo under the baseball cap, Will looks like a kid in a Disney movie. On the table a sign with flowery writing says, *These were a few of his favourite things.* Books: the whole set of the Black Stallion.

DVD: Happy Gilmour. Pack of baseball cards. Baseball glove. Bag of Doritos. Electric guitar. Haki sack, grey, with frayed threads. Justin feels as though he's wandered into the wrong room. Some other kid who died.

Then the chapel doors open and while they wait to file inside, Justin sees Amanda slip a rock onto the table. He absolutely is not going to ask her about it later. The chapel is packed. They sit in the back row, which is not nearly far enough away from all those people who look like aunts and uncles and cousins at the front. There are at least two other kids with wild blonde hair like Will's. He wonders if they knew what Will was really like. He wonders if he knew.

Justin doesn't try to sing along, but his mom and Amanda are right into the program. They're both pretty awful singers. A few words from an uncle, then a man who was Will's baseball coach, then a minister talks and then finally Will's dad steps up and thanks them all for coming. He starts to say that he knows Will must be smiling down at this wonderful gathering . . . and then he chokes up and walks back to his seat and the music begins for one last song.

While everyone else is making their way to the room with the coffee and trays of sweets, the three of them sign the guest book. Justin waits while his mother writes a message that uses up all the space beside their names and then runs down the margin of the page. He knows that on the way home she's going to ask him if he thought about it.

About what he would have said to Will if he'd known he wasn't ever going to see him again. He watches the murmuring guests in the reception room. Looks back at the kid in the picture on the table. At the plain grey haki sack.

A deep breath, and then he puts his shoulders back so that he feels much taller, and walks through the doorway to stand in front of Will's mom. "I'm Justin," he says. "Will sat in front of me this year. And last year too." The woman bites her lip and nods, and that's enough for both of them.

Amanda and his mom have followed him into the room, but he turns and leaves them there. Outside in the parking lot, he squints in the bright sunlight. What would he have said? Nothing, he'll tell her.

But then he takes out his haki sack. "Hey, Will," he whispers. "Wanna rally?" A couple of slow kicks, then heels and toes fly and he dances on his little patch of funeral home pavement. When his mom and Amanda finally come out the door, the hack still hasn't hit the ground.

Sisters

SARAH ELLIS

. . .

Mrs. Fenner's funeral was on the first day of spring. It was windy. The sky was a map of islands, grey and white, on a sea of washed-out blue. The islands dissolved and merged, continental drift in fast forward.

At the cemetery I stared hard at the clouds. I looked up to keep from looking at the ground, into the ground. Most of the words the minister said were cloud-words. Mercy, hope, peace, thin words whipped away by the wind. And a few earth-words. Ashes, blood, bread, grass. The grass at the cemetery was still yellow-dry from winter. The grave was a bright green box, lined with astroturf. Mrs. Fenner was the first person I knew who died. I think.

Afterwards I went home with Miss Poole and helped pass sandwiches. The guests were the minister, Mrs. Fenner's businessman son Robert, who flew in from Toronto, and some friends who live in Mrs. Fenner and Miss Poole's building. The sandwiches were ham or egg salad. Then there were butter tarts and ginger cookies. Mrs. Sutherland from 604 brought a pan of fudge squares. There was tea and sherry.

Robert Fenner poured out the sherry from a decanter shaped like a Scotsman with bow legs and a bright yellow and red kilt. His tartan tam was the stopper. Mrs. Fenner had made the decanter when she took up ceramics. She had also made frogs to hold hand soap and ceramic potatoes to hold sour cream. People talked a lot about all the things she had made. The things she had left behind. Then they all went away.

I should explain about Mrs. Fenner and Miss Poole. They are my foster grandmothers. I got them the year my sister Sophie ran away the first time. Mum and Dad thought I should have foster grandparents because my real ones live in Florida and France. They thought we needed more people in my family.

The foster-grandparent organizers sent us to meet three regular grandfather/grandmother pairs. One pair had a dog who liked me. One had a cottage in the mountains. "We could take you there in the summer if you'd like that, Charlotte." One had a lot of computer games. But I didn't want any of them to be my grandparents. When Mum asked me why, I said, "They look at me too hard." I was only nine. I didn't know how to say that they had a kind of hungry look, that they made me feel like a rent-a-kid.

And then we met Mrs. Fenner and Miss Poole, two sisters. The first time we visited them we all sat at the kitchen table with old magazines, scissors, glue and cardboard ice-cream buckets. Mrs. Fenner was into decoupage that year. The sisters talked to each other and to Mum. The words floated over my head as I cut and pasted. "I think young Charlotte has remarkable colour sense," Miss Poole said to Mrs. Fenner. Their fat cat Ditto jumped onto the table and overturned the glue. Miss Poole held him close to her face and growled at him. Mrs. Fenner showed me how to pick up tiny bits of paper by licking the end of my finger. We had tea and the afternoon disappeared. On the way home, hugging my decorated waste-paper basket, I told Mum that Mrs. Fenner and Miss Poole were my choice.

From then on I went over to their apartment lots of days after school. Sometimes the grans took me out. Fridays we went to early-bird bingo at the Catholic hall. Mrs. Fenner played eight cards at once and was calm even when she won. Miss Poole sat on the edge of her chair, talked to the numbers on her card and made mistakes.

The lady who gave out the bingo prizes was young and pretty, with red hair like Sophie. Sometimes I used to pretend she *was* Sophie and that one day she would peer down from the stage through the smoke and recognize me, her little sister. "Charlotte! Is that you?" Then she would come home with us for good, bringing all the bingo prizes. We would get on the bus carrying lamps and cookware sets and embroidered pillowcases and we would all laugh. I had strange ideas when I was nine and ten.

We all stopped going to Bingo when Mrs. Fenner's leg got bad. Mostly we just stayed in. I would sit at the kitchen table and crochet afghan squares and listen to them talk. The grans came from a village in England and they remembered all the people there. I got to know them, too. Addie's Harold, who was a right terror until they gave him a ferret to care for. "Mind you, it did take one aback when that little ferret face would peek out of his shirt." Stanley, who ran in the Empire Games. "It was a miracle. To think of him being that poor weak baby. Ada had to carry him around on a pillow with his little legs dangling over." And Jeannie who went off to London to become a dancer. "Aunt Effie went to see her, a surprise like, and they put her at a table right near the front and when Jeannie came out she didn't have a stitch on, just a few of them feathers. Well, Eff just didn't know where to look. Mind, she never told Jeannie's mum, it would have killed her."

When I got older Mum thought I went to visit the grans because I was being good. "It's so kind of you to go and see them," she said.

Kind had nothing to do with it. I went there to escape the

silence that was our house. I went there for the words. And for the people.

I went there for Addie's Harold and Stanley and the feathered Jeannie. I went there for mild Alf Minkin, who wouldn't say boo to a goose and then one day upped and pelted the grocer's van with two dozen eggs. For beautiful Emily, known as Pigeon, who fell in love five times in one year and threw herself down the well for the sixth. For Jack, who revealed his true nature that night in the badger blind and had to emigrate. For Alice, the grans' older sister who went a bit wild and ran off when she was a teenager. "And she landed on her feet, didn't she, Ida? I expect young Sophie will be just the same."

The grans talked about Sophie, even though they had never met her. I couldn't talk about her. Her name stuck in my throat.

But I didn't have to talk at the grans'. It was a place for listening. Best of all was listening to Miss Poole's stories of dead people. Car-accident victims who haunt certain highways, dead husbands who leave messages in the melting snow, indelible stains — "And they scrubbed and scrubbed but the kitchen floor would never come clean. Then one day they found an old scrapbook in the attic, filled with yellowing newspaper clippings. And there was the story, the grisly murder that had taken place years before, in that very house, in that very kitchen."

"Hush up, Ida, you're just flapping your tongue," Mrs.

Fenner would sometimes say when she remembered that I was a child and might be scared. Miss Poole never thought of that. I knew that she didn't think of me as a child. Just the way she didn't think of Ditto as a cat. She just talked. To people, animals, the radio, the kettle and the bunions on her feet. Anyway, I wasn't scared. Those were my favourite stories.

I continued to visit the grans because their apartment was full of people. They crowded onto the sofa, hung around the doorways, leaned against the fridge, sat on the floor hugging their knees to fit. There were babies on the bed with the coats, and little kids hiding under the table. People jostling, elbowing, stepping on the cat by mistake and talking, talking, talking. Noisy ghosts.

We have a ghost in our house, too. A silent ghost. The ghost of Sophie who came home once, twice, and never again, who last phoned five years ago. She floats around the house like a piece of empty air. They used to talk about her. They used to argue. Once I heard Dad yelling, "She's gone, Trish. Accept it." But now the Sophie ghost has silenced even my parents who never mention her.

Last Christmas, when I was helping Dad unpack the tree ornaments, he pulled out Sophie's stocking. He stared at it for a minute. I wanted to say something like, "I expect she landed on her feet." But the words couldn't push through the silence. Dad just packed the stocking back into the box and went outside to put up the lights. I think he forgot I was there. Sophie settles like fog on Christmas and birth-days and memories.

No, I'm not a citizen-of-the-week-teenager visiting the elderly. I go to the grans to keep from dissolving into a ghost myself.

After everyone had left I stayed to help Miss Poole tidy up. We took a few dirty dishes into the kitchen and then Miss Poole said, "Leave this for a minute. Come and sit down." I was surprised. Miss Poole likes to get jobs over and done with. And sitting is not her style. She is always jumping up to make tea or adjust the radio or water the African violets.

She perched on the edge of her chair. Ditto did a figure-of-eight around her feet. I glanced sideways quickly at Mrs. Fenner's armchair, the big one, hoping to catch someone in it. Mrs. Fenner or someone else. It was empty.

Miss Poole beat a little drum roll on her knees, reached into a patchwork pocket that hung over the arm of the chair and pulled out an envelope.

"Muriel left me a letter. I haven't told anyone about it yet, except Ditto. Didn't fancy discussing it with Robert, some-how. He's not much of a one for talk about the old days."

There was a large waiting feeling in the air.

"She wasn't my sister."

"What?"

"She was my aunt."

"Your aunt?" I couldn't figure it out. I've never been good

at that relative stuff, cousins once removed and all that.

Miss Poole gave the letter a sharp slap with the back of her hand.

"It's all there. Alice was my mother."

Alice. The other sister. Alice who was no better than she should be. Twice-divorced Alice who finally took off for America with a weedy little man who told her he was rich and, surprise of surprises, was. Alice who lived out her final days "eaten up with the cancer she was" in New Mexico on a hacienda or some such thing.

"You mean Alice who ran away?"

"The very one. Old toffee-nosed Alice." Miss Poole snorted. "She had me when she was fifteen. So the whole family upped and moved and when they got to the next place they just let on I was the new baby in the family. Mum took me on, just like she took on Uncle Harry when he started having his turns. And then Muriel and Mr. Fenner took me on when they came here to Canada. Isn't that a turn-up for the books?"

I was still having trouble with the generations. "So who was your mum?"

"Alice."

"No, I mean the one you call Mum."

"Well, she was really my grandmother. Look, come here." Miss Poole scribbled a diagram on the envelope. "Here's Mum. Two little lines down, that's Muriel and Alice, and from Alice one little line down to me."

"They never told you this?"

"It was the shame of it. With Dad being a churchwarden and all. And perhaps they thought it would give me a bad feeling about myself. One of those traumas they discuss on those television talk shows."

"And you never knew till now?"

Miss Poole leaned back in her chair a little and Ditto jumped into her lap. "Is there another cup in that pot?"

I poured out some thick-looking tea and handed it to her. "It's not very hot."

"But nice and strong. Just the way I like it." Miss Poole stared out the window for a minute. "The thing of it is, I did know. Not to say anything. And not the real truth. But I knew that I didn't match. All those Pooles. They were so big and calm. They kind of just set where you put them. But I was little and I couldn't sit still."

"Hyperactive?"

"Is that what they call it now? They wouldn't have me in school. I wouldn't stay in the desk. And meals. Father couldn't stand the fidgeting. Mostly I ate my dinner sitting on the step. The other thing was I was the wrong colour. Too brown. All those pink blonde people. Neighbours would comment on it and Mum used to say, 'That Ida, she does take the sun so.' Come to think of it now I suppose I took after my father. Whoever he was when he was at home."

Miss Poole took a gulp of tea and looked at the letter again.

"I'm not denying that it is a bit of a shock though. Perhaps not quite in the way that Muriel expected. The biggest thing is . . ." Miss Poole looked at me and grinned. "You'll be thinking I'm a dafty."

"No, I won't. What?"

"I always thought I was a fairy."

"What, with wings?"

"No, not that kind. A changeling. You don't know about them? You with all your algebra and computers." Miss Poole leaned over and punched me on the arm.

"Fairies want human children, so they steal them away and leave their own babies, changelings, in their place. It made perfect sense to me. Changelings are dark. I was dark. Changelings cry a lot. Mother told me what a difficult baby I had been, crying and grizzling and never sleeping through the night. I just tucked these things away in my head."

I thought of a little girl sitting on the stairs eating her dinner and thinking she was some weird kind of fairy. It made me want to hug Miss Poole. But she's not a hugger.

"Did you think you were a fairy even when you grew up?"

"Well I did and I didn't. Things got very busy when we emigrated, what with keeping the house going and taking care of Robert while Muriel and Mr. Fenner went out to work. I didn't think about it all that much, to tell you the truth. But I had it all tucked away. And sometimes . . . like, one time we had this boarder. We were having a hard time making ends meet and we took in boarders. And there was this one called Merv Butt and he was a great one for making beer. He tried to make beer out of everything. He even boiled down our Christmas tree that year to try to make spruce beer. And here I was, a great grown-up girl, as old as you, and I still thought that was proof."

"Proof? I don't get it."

"Because of trying to fool the changeling. Sometimes people could get their own babies back by tricking the changeling into revealing herself. They would act silly and try to get the changeling to speak. Like in one story the people boil water in an eggshell and the changeling baby sits up in the cradle and says, "I never in all my life saw water boiled in an eggshell." And then the changeling has to leave. So I thought that making beer out of a Christmas tree was the same thing. I was very careful not to act surprised."

"It sounds a bit lonely."

Miss Poole shook her head. "It wasn't that way. It made me feel strong. Magic, immortal, all of that good fairy stuff. And it explained things. Anyway, people do that all the time. Make themselves up. I mean, look at those movie stars. They take them out to Hollywood and glam them up and give then new names and make them famous. But I did it all by myself."

Miss Poole looked over at Mrs. Fenner's chair. "She was very good to me, was Muriel. Very good."

She absently pulled Ditto's ears. He broke into a loud rasping purr. "Who's my favourite boy?"

Then she suddenly sat forward, dumping Ditto. "Did we ever tell you about the time Muriel bought that goat at the fall fair? Well, you know how Muriel was not what you'd call a small woman? It seems that this goat . . ."

The phone rang. "Bother, that will be Olivia. I'll get it in the bedroom."

Olivia was Robert's wife. According to the grans, if you put your drink next to her it would stay cool all evening.

I picked up some dirty dishes, took them into the kitchen and piled them by the sink. I looked out the window. The clouds parted and the sun angled into the room, throwing a shadow of the frog soap-dish onto the fridge. I sent my mind out to the cemetery where Mrs. Fenner was. The trees and the tombstones would be making long shadows. I held up two fingers and gave the frog antennae. Ditto leaned against my leg and I thought about the different kinds of gone. I wondered about Mrs. Fenner and the goat. I thought about remembering, naming and telling.

Miss Poole bustled into the kitchen and made a horrible face. "She wants me to come and visit for Christmas. Very kind and all but I can't imagine anything more dismal. I'm thinking that I had better make some plans to protect myself. There's a seniors' bus trip to Edmonton on before Christmas. The West Edmonton Mall, now that's something I'd like to see before I turn up my toes."

I held my hands in the sunlight and made a butterfly flutter across the fridge.

Miss Poole smiled. "That's lovely."

My sister. I wanted to say her name, to have it exist in the room, in the light and the shadows.

"Sophie taught me. She was really good at shadows because she was sort of double-jointed. She could bend her thumbs right back and gross people out."

"Oh, I know the feeling. There was a boy in the village, the youngest Crank boy, Sid. He could practically turn himself inside out. Made you sick to look at him, but you *did* look, all the same."

I suddenly remembered Sophie and me in a tent at night. I was holding the flashlight and Sophie was making huge looming shadows on the canvas walls. The terror was delicious.

I stuck my fingers out at odd angles and created another shadow. "Do you know what that is?"

"Haven't a clue."

"It's a Blob-Dog, Guardian of the Underworld. He was one of Sophie's best ones. The other good one was Angel-Lips, High School Queen."

Miss Poole grinned. "That Sophie sounds a right caution."

A right caution. I wasn't sure what it meant, but it had a Sophie-feeling about it. Did I ever tell you about my sister? She was a *right caution.*

Miss Poole picked up a pink rosebud teacup. It was smeared with chocolate where the fudge square had melted against it. "That always happens when you have chocolate things at a tea. Seems like such a waste. I'll tell you a secret. After Muriel got beyond helping in the kitchen, I invented my own method of clean-up, very sensible it is, too."

Miss Poole held the cup up to her mouth, stuck out her tongue and licked it clean. She handed me a cup. "Try it. This is likely the way fairies wash up."

My cup was forest green with a thin gold band. The chocolate was rich and the china was cool and both were smooth, smooth under smooth. We licked the cups clean like a pair of cats, and from the living room came a quiet hum of stories, cloud-words and earth-words and the voices of the not-gone.

Explaining Andrew

GINA ROZON

. . .

L ast night Andrew trashed his room. Totally. He knocked football-sized holes in the walls searching for spy cameras. Dad was out — he's out a lot lately — and Mum stood in the hall with her hand over her mouth, crying. Andrew calmed down after I went in there and pretended to find the master control, a pen, a Pilot V Grip, fine, and "disabled" it. I smashed it with the base of his old bowling trophy. Andrew destroyed the little bronze bowler two weeks ago, because the "enemy" bugged it to monitor his brain waves.

"He saw us." It's a hiss, insistent, urgent, so close the hair by my ear trembles in the breath released with the words.

I hunch my shoulders and duck my head to shake him off. Then I fake an interest in the worn *Reader's Digest* in my hands. I had grabbed it off the top of a lopsided pile on the end table when I sat down. All the reading material in Dr. Muehlenberg's waiting room is old, but I don't care. Anything that gives me an excuse to ignore Andrew will do. I flip open the magazine and there's this article called "Adding up the Good Things." I wish I had some good things to add up.

Andrew, upset I shrugged off his warning, twitches. An unlit cigarette flips between the fingers of his right hand. He itches to be out of here to smoke it. If he can con Mum out of the money, he always has one lit. He'll follow her around the house for half an hour going, "Five bucks, Mum? You got five bucks? Just five bucks, Mum? Can I have five bucks? Five bucks, Mum? Come on, Mum. I need a smoke, Mum. You got five bucks?" She'll give him the five bucks just to shut him up — if Dad isn't home to stop her.

When he can't get five bucks out of Mum, he still manages to get cigarettes. Begging them off people on the street if he has to. He's . . . menacing, scary. Former friends hand over their entire pack and bolt. It's as though what went wrong with his brain has morphed out to his face and twisted it too. People cross the street when they see him. Heck, if he weren't my brother *I'd* cross the street.

Andrew looks like a grimy panhandler. We can't get him to shower; he thinks the stall is rigged. Once some idiot dropped a loonie into his ball cap when Andrew just happened to take it off his head. So he's always holding it out, ready for another drop of metal sympathy. He knows people feel sorry for him, like Mum does.

As far as I'm concerned, sympathy just encourages his behaviour, but nobody listens to me — nobody except Andrew, that is. I'm the one person he will listen to — the kid brother who used to follow him everywhere. I'm seventeen and I still go everywhere with him because I'm the babysitter now. I try to be good-natured about it because he suffered my kid-brother company all those years. But I wasn't half as hard to put up with. For one thing, I didn't scare all his friends away.

"We need to find a safe house when we leave," Andrew demands, peevish because I ignored him. He says it to the empty seat beside him. Andrew does things like that, talks to people who aren't there. "He's relayed our position to his partner. No! The old place won't be safe. I said no!"

The "old place" means our house. Where does he think he'll go? None of the people who used to like him want him around anymore. Not even our relatives. Hard on the heels of a dinner invitation, comes, "I'm sorry, I'm not sure how to put this, this is hard, but we think it would be better if you didn't bring Andrew." Guess who stays home and watches Andrew while Mum and Dad go for dinner?

On the far side of the empty seat — the one Andrew is berating — sits a woman wearing dark green overalls, the kind Dad used to wear down at the machine shop. An oval white badge embroidered with blue thread identifies her as "Jenny." Three fingers on her left hand are wrapped with white gauze. Jenny Osgood, the only female welder in town. Looks like she slipped up.

Jenny and Andrew were in the same class right from kindergarten to grade twelve. They played trumpet side-by-side for high school band. During grade twelve, they went out together for all of two weeks but Andrew said they'd been friends too long to be anything else. I don't think Jenny agreed. She still came over to the house to hang out, but you could see she wasn't happy. And then Andrew changed. We haven't seen Jenny around for ages.

Jenny sees me and looks away. Andrew's monologue must embarrass her because she edges out of her seat and moves to the empty spot on the other side of the end table. Putting the mounds of ancient history between her and me. And Andrew. I think for a minute she'll say hello to me and I realize I don't want her to.

Conversations with people who knew us before are awkward. Like our whole family came down with some embarrassing disease, herpes maybe, and friends don't know what to say. They can't think of anything besides Andrew and his "problem" and we don't want to talk about that. It's hard enough just to live with it.

Jenny picks up one of the newer *Digests* (February 2002: "Will the Hospital Make You Sick?"), and reads. Or pretends to. I'm relieved she'll ignore us after all, and then depressed.

These days, Dad and Mum argue all the time about putting Andrew in the hospital. Mum says she can't put her child "away." Dad says, "They won't 'put him away.' He'll get the help he needs. And look what it's doing to James. Doesn't he deserve some freedom, too?" Dad knows.

Andrew doesn't trust Mum, you see, and she can't handle him when he spouts off on the conspiracy stuff, so it has to be me. It's always me.

When Mum turns and asks me if it's *really* too much trouble to look after him, voice pleading, I can't tell her it is. Even though it is. I just know she'd cry for hours and hate me forever. But maybe that would be okay. Could I live with Mum's tears and hate easier than I can live with being Andrew's keeper forever and ever?

I'm at the right place to take care of it, too. Months ago Dr. Muehlenberg said it's time. Andrew needs a thorough assessment. He said it like an auto mechanic says the van needs a major tune-up. And the place to do it is in the hospital. He's not qualified to deal with this. Neither am I. Mum's wrong to think so.

If I work this right, I could go home alone. Today. What would Mum say if I did? Oh, I can just hear her. "James, how *could* you? When you know how I feel about it? That's *so* unlike you! What *were* you thinking?"

Andrew nudges me with his elbow, nods his head towards

his friend, the empty orange vinyl seat, and says, "He'll defend us on the way out, if necessary. He's a ninja." His voice drops and I know he's afraid. "Of course, you never know who to trust. Do you think they sent him to get me?"

Out of the corner of my eye I see Jenny glance towards us, then her eyes dart back to the *Digest*. I shake my head no, for Andrew, and try to focus on the article I'm still pretending to read. A quote jumps off the page. "I realized I could look at my life from another angle: When faced with adversity I could ask 'What's the good in it?'"

Mum doesn't come to the doctor's office with us any more. She can't bear it. The last three times we've brought Andrew, Dr. Muehlenberg's phoned her afterwards and recommended the hospital. For special care, he calls it. Mum won't do it. Today she wants me to ask about another drug. Something to calm him down. Dr. Muehlenberg told her it's not that simple. But she doesn't seem to hear him.

I try to concentrate on the article again. It's hopeless. On the facing page — opposite the "Finding good in adversity" quote, the three little pigs (huge open-mouthed smiles on their pudgy cartoon faces) drive a shiny red Ford Windstar past a tree. Behind the tree, the Big Bad Wolf stands, drooling. The ad says, "Who's afraid of the big, bad commute?" I don't get the point. Is the Windstar supposed to save the pigs or is the Big Bad Wolf drooling because he sees an easy meal of ham in a can?

Maybe I'll get myself committed instead of Andrew.

The receptionist calls my name and motions for us to come. Andrew gets up, glances once over his shoulder at the middle-aged guy by the outer door, beer belly hanging over the waist of his black jeans — the "him" who saw us — and hurries after the receptionist. I take the *Digest* with me. Sometimes we wait a while in the examining room, too. Andrew thinks we're here for the doctor to see me — a ploy the doctor and his staff play out. A ruse to get Andrew here.

Dr. Muehlenberg has been our family doctor forever — since Andrew was born. He's short, with hairy arms and a thick beard. He looks like the guy who played Santa Claus in the old *Miracle on 34th Street* movie, the one with Natalie Wood as the kid who doesn't believe in Santa. He arrives with a thick folder of papers and a smile that doesn't reach his eyes. No miracles here.

"James, Andrew," he says. "And what can I do for you today?"

"James still has a sore throat," Andrew volunteers. "Mum says he needs some new medicine."

"New medicine, eh?" Dr. Muehlenberg pretends to peer down my throat. I've had this sore throat for six months. He tosses the wooden tongue depressor into the garbage, makes a note in the file folder. I wonder just what he writes in there each month. His shopping lists maybe? "So James, how's your mother these days?"

"The same."

It's like a code we've come up with, Dr. Muehlenberg and

I. The funny thing is, with all his conspiracy theories and invisible people, Andrew hasn't figured out my persistent sore throat is mighty fishy.

"And the rest of the family?"

"Well, I think I'd be better if someone at the hospital had a look. Dad thinks so, too." There. I've said it. Dr. Muehlenberg looks away, makes another note. Does he get the message? Does he understand things are worse than ever? "And Andrew thinks one of your patients is spying on him. The guy by the door, with the black jeans."

"It's okay, it's okay, James knows what he's doing," Andrew instructs the empty air beside him, palms outward like he has to calm somebody down. I wonder if it's the ninja. Andrew puts the cigarette in and out of his mouth like it's already lit. Puffing.

Dr. Muehlenberg assures Andrew the guy is just Tom Watts, the laundromat manager. Of course, Andrew doesn't believe him. Dr. Muehlenberg gets the same look he always gets when he talks to Andrew. Regretful. Disappointed. He scratches behind his right ear, pen in hand.

"Your mother won't like it," he says. "But you know I agree."

"It's the best way to make my sore throat go away, right?" I don't want to think about this anymore. I just want to make it happen. Get Andrew to the hospital. Is it the right thing, though? I mean — Mum won't think so. Can I do this? How can I? The *Reader's Digest* weighs a ton and I drop it on the examining table. On the cover stark white letters on a black background declare: "Hostage to Allah's Madmen." That's what it feels like. I'm a hostage.

Andrew makes a choked, air-sucking noise. I look up and he's backed into the corner, on his toes with his ass almost in the sink, and he's pointing at Dr. Muehlenberg, horrified. Oh man, now what? Then he starts to holler, "Get it! Get it! Disable it, quick!" Disable the doctor? How do I disable a person? No, it's not Dr. Muehlenberg — it's something in his hand. The pen. A Pilot V Grip, fine. Of course. Dr. Muehlenberg turns to me (I am so tired of people expecting me to explain Andrew).

"The pen."

Dr. Muehlenberg gets it right away. He hands me the pen but then I'm kind of stuck — it's not like Dr. Muehlenberg keeps busted trophies around to smash master control spy devices. I try to decide what to do, so Andrew will stop freaking out. Then Andrew drops his cigarette and grabs the two stirrup-shaped metal things out of the end of the examining table. He stands there and holds them like he's an outlaw, ready to shoot it out with the sheriff. I figure he'll knock some pretty good holes in the wall with the stirrups and I get an idea.

I throw the pen on the counter beside the sink. "Hit it with one of those!"

Andrew hits the pen a bunch of times, smashes it to bits with Dr. Muehlenberg's examining table stirrup. By the time the receptionist knocks and sticks her head in to ask if everything is okay, the pen is a wreck and there's black ink all over the metal stirrup and on the counter but Andrew's calm. He must be satisfied he's destroyed it. Dr. Muehlenberg says everything's fine and the receptionist, no fool, shakes her head and leaves.

"I'll phone your dad. He'll meet you at the hospital and we'll arrange those tests," Dr. Muehlenberg says. Like nothing has happened and we're still talking about my sore throat. He's looking at me, but I know he means tests for Andrew. This sounds corny, but it's like this huge weight came right off my shoulders. I'm that relieved to hear him say it.

Andrew wasn't far off thinking there's a conspiracy, after all. But the plot is between Dr. Muehlenberg and me. It has nothing to do with the laundromat manager or the invisible ninja or the group bugging Andrew's room to read his brain waves while he sleeps. It has everything to do with the schizophrenia shooting around his brain cells and turning him from my laid-back and likeable (for a brother) brother into somebody I wouldn't want to meet on the street in broad daylight, let alone after dark. Somebody I'm so relieved to be rid of.

I'd like to ask the lady who wrote the *Reader's Digest* article on adversity: "Where's the good in this?"

Cold Snap

DIANA ASPIN

. . .

I saw my dad and the other woman when I went to my friend Anna's house to work on an astronomy assignment. Neutrinos.

"Come on, Cassie." Anna pulled at my sleeve.

I was on Anna's porch, tugging off my boots. In the driveway opposite a man who looked like my dad pulled a woman to him, rough and hungry, like in the movies, then let her go. It was my dad! As I stood there a girl I recognized from grade twelve appeared. She was blonde and pretty. Very pretty. She kissed her mom hello, then touched my dad's arm briefly before going inside.

I shook Anna off me and stepped outside. I watched my

dad leave, his collar up against the wind, his brown, wavy hair flying in all directions. His strong plumber's hands stuffed deep in his pocket, he bounced down the road, hopped into our Ford pickup and roared off.

I said over and over to myself: there *has* to be a mistake. I knew all about affairs, but they were things that happened to other kids' parents. My dad was a *family* man; everyone knew that. Dependable Ted Skinner. Call him any time day or night and he'd help out. He coached peewee hockey, he organized Baysville's boat show, and he curled. He grew African violets for Chrissake. Guys who grew African violets didn't mess with other women!

Anna shook my arm. "Cassie! A hundred trillion neutrinos whistle through *your* body every second!"

All that whistled through *my* body was the thought: who was that woman? My arms and legs felt numb, as if they didn't belong to me.

I'm called Cassie because my dad is a star freak. Some nights, once the lake is safely frozen, we lie on it, ogle the stars, and talk. Dad would have liked to call me Cassiopeia, because he's into Greek legends — King Cepheus, the Oracle and all that. But he thought I'd get teased. People think it's short for Cassandra, which is a neat name, but, as my dad says, nothing to do with the stars.

That night, curled up in bed, I thought about my friend, Reena. How her dad just upped and left without a trace when she was five. I thought about Paige, about how her dad did a runner and was never heard from again. How now, almost always, her mom is smashed. And Emma, whose dad was in the slammer. I'd had more good times with my dad than Reena. My dad was not an armed robber. And I couldn't imagine my mom turning into a boozer because my dad took off. But who knew? I never could imagine *this* happening either.

For two days following my sighting, Dad was up at Kawagama Lake playing poker with his buddies. This gave me time to raid his closet. In our house we never nosed around in each other's belongings, but I figured that as far as he was concerned that was passé. I could play sneaky, pig-faced cheat, too.

I wasn't sure what I was looking for in Dad's closet, a clue maybe. I dug about in the pockets of his pants and came up with some receipts — no love letters or lipsticky tissues. My fingers shook as I pulled out the sleeve of the old denim shirt he wore when he was doing odd jobs about the house, or tending his precious violets. I lifted the sleeve and stuck my face in it, hauled in air. A mix of stale sweat, and a musky scent that was exactly him. A feeling I'd lost something stirred inside me. I stared at the sleeve; it was flat, shapeless and empty.

After I saw Dad with that woman, after I thought of him spending time with *her,* instead of with Mom, spending time with that pretty girl instead of *me,* I saw in the bathroom mirror a girl who was disposable. My dad was not who I thought he was. He was a nasty low-down snake in the grass, a two-timing, double-crossing adulterer.

The other thing I did, a few days later, was follow the girl home after school. And guess what! Dad's Ford was parked close by. He wasn't fixing burst pipes in Barrie after all. He was with *them.*

"Hi, Cassie," my dad said the following night. He popped his head around the door of my room on the way to his. Under my bare feet the floor vibrated with sound. The alternative music shook my shelves, rattled my bones, and kept me so livid I thought I'd implode like some giant star.

I pretended not to hear him. I kept rubbing at some blood-red nail polish, driving the reddened remover into the clumps of chewed-up skin around my cuticle. I liked the way it stung.

"I said: Hi, Cassie." Imagining himself welcome, he sat down.

I smashed the bottle down on my bedside table. Remover shot all over the wall. I rolled my eyes and rubbed furiously at my thumbnail.

"Look what you've done!" Dad jumped up. "What's gotten into you?" He left, came back with a wet cloth and dabbed at the wall.

"Talk to me, Cassie," Dad said. "Or is it a girl thing?"

"Sort *of!*" I shouted, spit flying.

Dad had a worried crease in the centre of his forehead, between his eyebrows, like a "V." In the Old Days if I saw his worried "V," I teased him out of it. "Dear King Cepheus," I said. "Take me to the Oracle!" I tossed my long hair about like the Queen I thought I was. Mom often said that I was my dad's daughter, not hers, one reason being my hair. It was dark brown and wavy, just like his, so long I could sit on it. It was our — Dad's and my — pride and joy.

Dad plucked at his beard. "What gives, Cassie?"

I yanked my eyebrows into a bored arch. "Anything you want to tell *me*, Dad?"

"Like what?"

I glared up at him. His "V" had deepened; he *really* didn't get it. He *really* thought he could do this to us and get away with it.

Liar. Cheat. Pig. Let him suffer and die.

In the end he just barked, "I give up!"

"And don't call me Cassie," I screamed after him. "I hate that name! I *hate* it!"

"Your brother tells me you lost it with Dad last night." Mom sat on their bed, tugging on her white stockings. "Want to tell me about it?"

I shook my head.

Mom slipped her feet into her white shoes and laced them. "Ugly uniform," she said. She pulled down her slip and examined herself sideways in the mirror. Mom was — still is — an emergency room nurse. She ran her hand over her tummy, patted it as she would a friendly dog. "Not what it used to be," she said, kind of wistfully.

True, Mom's tummy wasn't what it used to be. She used to be thin as a blade of grass. Though if you asked me, I thought she looked better this way; it was the kind of tummy a kid or a dog could lay its head on and be very very content. *The pretty plumping out she was doing, that couldn't be why he was messing around, could it?*

Over the next few days, when I wasn't in school, or freezing my buns off walking home from the bus, I lived in my room. I read, played CD's, and chased away thoughts about the blonde woman and her daughter. I saw my dad, having dumped us, leaning across their kitchen table, his shoulder brushing the daughter's as he helped her with math. I saw her smile up at him — the kind of sickeningly white smile you see on the covers of magazines.

Later, my imaginings got so bad that I fished my old bear, Arnold, out of the closet. I tucked my knees to my chest and pulled Arnold's head up under my throat, pressed his torn heart against mine. I cried until my head ached. Then I stuffed Arnold back into the closet, kicked the door closed, and filled myself back up with the coolest and deadliest weapon of all time: HATE.

A few days later things came to a head. My dad promised he'd be home early so we could go lie out on the lake. Big Deal! I'd rather have hacked my right arm off at the elbow.

At seven-thirty he called. "Oh," Mom said, "well, see you in the morning then." And to me: "Your dad has work in Barry's Bay."

I stared at the TV, my heart beating.

"Finished your project with Anna?"

I shrugged. I didn't plan on reading one more *word* about neutrinos. Neutrinos would forever be a dirty word. I wanted an "F" on my astronomy project — see how he liked that.

I fumed. Mom was always looking after things: us, her plants, her patients, the neighbours. A pain needled its way into my chest and came out just between my shoulder blades. I thought I might throw up. Great, I thought. Her husband is spending the night with that cow while her daughter has a quadruple heart attack.

"What is it?" Mom asked. "Are you ill?"

Then I got this flash of Dad helping that pretty blonde girl with her math and something inside me heaved and burst open.

"Nothing," I yelled, taking the stairs two at a time. I called a friend to drive me to the woman's house. My sick heart thumped as I snatched a carton of eggs from the fridge and some nice sharp scissors from the kitchen drawer.

I crouched down behind a snowcapped bush. My first egg spun toward the woman's window. A hit! I fired another and another, the hate rising up my throat like bile until I thought I would choke on it.

Pig! Liar! One egg after another. Cheat! Die! Until the door opened.

The woman my dad had kissed so greedily stepped out until she was standing under the porch light. She pulled her sickly pink sweater about her and stared at the smashed eggs plastered across her windows and door. "What on earth . . . ?" If I'd had an egg left I'd have thrown it at her.

"What is it?" Dad's voice.

"Look, Ted!"

Ted! The family wrecker's voice rose an octave and broke on the word "look." I loved it, that breaking sound. I wanted all of her to break.

My dad wore blue jeans and his best brown corduroy shirt; he must have sneaked them out of the house. He looked and acted as though he lived there. Things were worse than I thought. It would take a miracle to get him back. And I didn't do miracles. I did "rage."

"Who'd do a thing like that?" Dad stared at the carpet of eggshells and the gooped-up door.

I jumped up from behind the snowy bush. "Me!"

I waited for him to rocket down the porch steps and shake me until I rattled, but he just stood there, frozen under the light. They both did. The woman had large eyes, but that could have been fear.

I stood my ground and waited for my dad to make a move.

"Go on in, Daisy," he said to her.

Daisy! It sounded like a goat!

For a moment I thought the woman was going to speak to me, but she put her hand across her fat mouth, went inside, and tossed out his coat.

"Bitch!" I yelled, surprising myself. I was losing it — and it sizzled.

My dad slumped onto the porch steps. He placed his head in his hands. "It's nothing to do with you, Cassie."

"She's an ugly cow!"

He looked up and I knew, even though there was a whole world of dark driveway and bush between us, that there was a deep "V" between his eyebrows.

"Cassie . . ." he began.

I screamed, "She's a fat pig," so loud it hurt my throat. I wanted to run over and tear his hair out. If I'd had a gun I'd have shot him. I didn't do "rage" anymore, I did Greek Legend Revenge Rage. I wanted to yell something obscene about the girl but I knew I'd cry if I did that. And I wasn't going to give him, or those bitches, that satisfaction.

I curled my toes up in my boots but tears came anyway. "I hate you! You're a . . . you're a . . ." I pulled my fists up level with my ears and shook them. "You're a baaaastard!" I screamed for so long that a door somewhere opened then shut again.

"Oh god, Cassie," my dad groaned.

I knelt and groped around under the bush for the egg box. I'd suddenly remembered that there was a cracked egg glued to it. I eased it out and hurled it. It struck his shoulder and burst open, yolk and shell sliding down his arm.

Then I took out the kitchen scissors. "See these?"

"Put those down!"

"Why should I do anything *you* tell me to?"

Before he could reach me, I dragged a handful of hair from under the collar of my coat, tipped my head to one side, and chopped off a great hunk close to my ear. The sound of the blunt scissors chewing through my hair made a sort of grinding noise; I half-expected it to hurt but it didn't. My whole life I'd been growing it. Dad was nuts about it. I grabbed another handful but he seized my wrist and shook the scissors roughly into the snow.

"Get your filthy hands off me!" I dropped to my knees, sobbing, then leapt up with the scissors.

"Give me those!"

But he didn't scare me. I plunged the scissors at him a few times before stuffing them into my pocket so fiercely I heard the lining rip. "And don't you *dare* follow me."

I took off, a slight breeze shifting the ice-slicked tree branches, rattling them like tin foil. I ran, sobbing, toward my friend's car. I tripped headfirst on a mound of ice. I grazed my palms as I slid along the ground. I heard Dad shouting at the top of his lungs for me and then he stopped.

"Cassie!" Mom scrambled up, her sewing basket spilling pins, buttons and thread. She flipped my hands and stared at my bloody palms. "What happened? Oh! Your hair!" She reached out to touch it but I shrank back. I couldn't bear to be touched, even by her. I smelled raw eggs, and tasted vomit at the back of my throat.

When Mom realized she'd get nothing out of me, and I'd assured her I hadn't been attacked, she became her efficient self. She ushered me into the shower. When I came out she wrapped me in a warmed towel and tidied my hacked-up hair. It was a brush-cut by the time she'd evened it out. When she was done, she tucked me into bed with a hot water bottle and arranged the covers so that only my nose poked out. "Talk later," she said, kissing the tip of it.

Where had my anger gone? I *liked* my anger. I gritted my teeth and chanted the really foul but satisfying F-word but all I could dredge up was big-time sad. Empty, like that sleeve in Dad's closet. I closed my eyes, saw my dad and that girl again. Outside, on the lake, ice shifted and I heard the familiar boom-boom from beneath it, like a cannon being fired. I got up, crept into the kitchen and, one by one, rolled the precious heads of his African violets between my fingers. Then I finished them off by watering them with a salt solution, and strode out onto the lake.

It was silent except for the odd crack or boom. I arched my neck, narrowed my eyes so hard the stars blurred and trembled, then I screamed. One throat-ripping, ear-piercing scream. Then, my face still hot from screaming, I lay down on my back and folded my arms across my chest. I hammered my heels into the snow until they hurt. I thought I was getting my temper back until a tear slid from my eye and trickled into my right ear.

"Cassie?" Dad's voice.

"Go away!" I tugged my hat down; my almost-bald head was freezing.

When he didn't speak, I looked up. Dad stood beside me, staring up into the night sky. Breath poured from his mouth, his dark, curly hair and bushy beard were crusted with ice, and his head was nestled in the stars. The whole world was iced over. Dad sat down next to me.

The expression "crock of shit" came to my mind, an expression I'd heard many times but never used. I had become the Queen of Dirty Words. So I said, "What a crock of *shit* this is."

I stared up at Cassiopeia, five stars in the shape of a W or an M. They used to be magic. I whispered the stars' names over and over to blot out my dad's ugly presence and my own foul mouth: Epsilon, Delta, Gamma, Alpha, Beta, Epsilon, Delta . . . If this had been an ordinary February night, I would have told him about the miracle of neutrinos, the way a hundred trillion were raging through his body every single second. But no way. Not now. Not *ever*.

"Cassie," my dad said. "It's over."

I resisted the urge to jump up and sock him in the jaw. "Over! How can it ever be over! *You* should know that! You're the grown-up — ha ha ha! If things could be over, bang, just because someone said so, we'd have no wars, would we! No poor people begging on the street! Dumb-ass!"

Eventually, because he refused to leave, I dragged myself to my feet. He stood up, too. I took him by surprise when I swung my boot back and kicked him in the calf. Then again. And again. I made a fist and pounded his chest. "Cheat!" I sobbed. "Pig!"

Dad reached out and ripped off my hat. He stared, unblinking at my hair. Then he took his own warm red hat, pulled it down over my hair and cheeks, held it against them with his big plumber's hands. He held it there for what seemed like forever.

An earlier version of "Cold Snap" was included in Diana Aspin's collection *Ordinary Miracles* (Red Deer Press, 2003)

the sign for heaven

CARRIE MAC

. . .

Lily wasn't deaf, but she needed to learn sign language. She couldn't speak because of the tracheotomy hole in her neck that helped her to breath. She was three when we met, and I was thirteen. She was a little brown-skinned girl with skinny legs and a round belly in a house full of blonde, tanned children, including Hans, the boy in my grade all the girls had a crush on, including me. He pretended getting Lily was no big deal, but I knew he was excited about it. She was going to be his new sister, his family's new little girl. While they were waiting for the adoption to be finalized, Lily and Hans and the rest of the family were learning sign language, and it was my job to teach them. The first sign I taught them was my name sign, *Della,* because I wanted Hans to use it, but he never did. He was an awkward signer, left-handed and clumsy.

I went to their house every Thursday after school, when we were all supposed to play together, using signs. Hans was too cool to "play," so he usually slouched against the wall with a comic book. The other kids dutifully played for a while, but lost interest quickly, because Lily was three years younger than the youngest of them. The father would suddenly remember some important task in his workshop, and the mother often drifted upstairs to bake cookies or start dinner. And then it was just Lily and me, and sometimes the family's other adopted child, eighteen-year-old Teddy, who had Down's Syndrome and a special talent for singing show tunes.

Lily was a fast learner. Her little fingers wrapped around signs like *play,* and *stop, more, drink, eat, no, yes.* Sometimes her mother brought us a snack, and Lily would look up to me for the sign before we ate: *carrots, crackers, cheese, peanut butter, apple.* Once it was hot chocolate, which became her favourite sign for awhile.

After a few months, the family asked me to go to church with them, so Lily could learn church signs. I dressed up and walked there the next Sunday, hoping to sit beside Hans, but he sat way over on the other side with a bunch of boys. The service was in German so I didn't understand any of it and neither did Lily. When Lily got bored she pulled me outside to the playground at the base of a towering carved cross. Teddy followed us out, and I taught them signs for *tree, street, church, God, bird, cross* while Teddy sang *New York, New York* so loudly that one of the elders came out to hush him up.

Earlier that summer I'd been to bible camp. On the bumpy bus ride along the dirt road to where the Jesus-horse-archery-marshmallow festivities would take place, I doubted anyone would be my friend. I was pretty sure everyone would find out I was a charity case whose single mom with a debt problem couldn't pay my way, and I thought it highly unlikely that I'd go the week without being called fat or four-eyes or both. I was sure of one thing though. I firmly and absolutely believed in God. I believed God was all seeing, all knowing, alternately great and kind, or grumpy and prone to punishment. I believed God was forgiving though, and open to negotiating through prayers that included promises of undying kindness to the elderly if only He would make Hans know I was alive. My prayers weren't always answered but I forgave Him for that. Hans might not know I was alive, but I did get to spend every Thursday afternoon at his house — which was more than I could say for any of the other girls in my class — fat, four-eyed or not.

When God didn't come through for me, I figured He was busy with something more pressing, such as lifting a child just dead from malnutrition or cholera in Africa up to heaven, or showing his wrath to a thief who'd just snatched a tottery old lady's purse by arranging for him to be hit by a bus. I was not a demanding believer, but I believed, nonetheless.

That Sunday in the playground under the cross, I asked Teddy if he believed in God.

"Yeah I do." He rubbed his thumb and first finger together. He only did that when he was nervous, so I figured maybe he didn't understand the question.

"Then what does God mean?" I asked.

"Heaven," he said in his thick, nasally voice. "Love."

"And?"

"Heaven. I said it already."

Lily tugged on my sleeve and pointed to the sky, eyebrows raised.

"You want to know the sign for heaven?"

She nodded.

But I didn't know the sign for heaven.

"God is up in it." Teddy thrust a chubby finger at the sky. "Up in it there."

Lily was waiting. I didn't want to admit that I didn't know the sign for heaven. I thought I should know it, considering my deep, devoted love of God.

"What does God look like?" I asked Teddy, trying to ignore Lily.

"Like in the pictures, silly."

"Does He talk to you?" A girl at camp, who said she was thinking about maybe being my friend, said that retards get special treatment from God. I told her not to call them retards, and she changed her mind about being my friend. But I was still curious about the special treatment. Teddy furiously rubbed this thumb and finger as he walked away.

"Teddy? Does He talk to you?"

Teddy shrugged.

"What does He say?"

Teddy shrugged again. Did that mean that yes, God did talk to him? Or did that mean no, He didn't?

"Teddy! Wait up!" I ran after him. "Does He? Does He really talk to you?"

"Hafta do Sunday school now."

Teddy lifted Lily into his arms and carried her inside to the basement, where the kids were gathering. I tried to stand beside Hans as we formed a circle, but Lily butted between us. They prayed in German and I prayed silently, in English, that Hans would wake up the next day and want to marry me.

"Do you understand German?" I asked Lily after the prayers as we glued painted macaroni to cardboard cutout crosses.

She shook her head. Renata, the youngest of her soon-to-be sisters leaned over. "She understands some of it, but we mostly talk English to her."

As Renata followed her friends out to the playground, I

whispered to Lily, "If you ever do start to understand German, and you hear Hans talk about me, you tell me, okay?"

She nodded, but I don't think she had a clue what I was going on about.

The adoption was finalized just before Lily's fourth birthday. The celebration invitations were in German and English, and there was a little drawing in the corner that Renata had done, of the sign for *I love you*. I don't know if Lily understood what was happening, but the blonde siblings (three sisters and four brothers) each gave her a gift, and a hug, and then they sang a song in German that the mom and dad had written for her. Then they sang it in English, and Teddy joined in, singing the words from some Broadway musical that had nothing to do with anything.

Lily met her new grandparents for the first time. One set came from Ontario, and the other set came all the way from Germany. They sat her on their laps and bounced her around like she was younger than she really was. That was easy to do, because she'd been a preemie baby addicted to drugs, and so she was much smaller than most kids her age. She signed *stop, off, no,* but they didn't know what she was trying to say, and I didn't feel like I should tell them, considering I was just some volunteer kid and they didn't speak much English anyway. Renata finally saw, and scolded them in German.

"I told them she's not a baby," she said after Lily was set down and had fled from the room in tears.

"She's overwhelmed," said her mother, and then she said something in German, probably repeating herself. "What's the sign for overwhelmed, Della?"

I showed them, starting with fists at the front of my face, and then opening them fast as I moved them past my ears.

"Like everything coming at you all at once."

Sometimes it made it easier for them if I could tag some little reminder to the sign, like the sign for *girl,* dragging your right thumb along your right jawbone, like a little girl's bonnet string.

They all tried it, even the grandparents. Lily came back into the room, stopping abruptly when she saw us all making the same sign.

That mean? she signed.

"Overwhelmed," I said.

Don't understand.

"Let's not worry, *liebling.*" Her new mother kissed her on the cheek. "It's a grown-up word. Come now, time for cake."

I went to church with them again at Easter, to teach Lily more churchy signs. The minister intoned in German, which made the sermon sound extra serious and cautionary, almost scary. As if God were in a bad mood that day and it was the minister's job to convey that to us.

"It's not scary at all," Renata said down in the basement

as we all ate hot cross buns and drank apple juice. "It's the same Jesus who died for our souls and then was given eternal life story, only in German."

"Still, it sounded pretty scary." My church was a happy-clappy church, where no one talked about hell. We had a real band, with electric guitars and a drum set, and we could wear whatever we wanted, even sneakers and jeans.

Lily brought over a book, open to a picture of an angel lifting a dead soldier up to heaven. He was bloody, the battleground beneath him strewn with the wounded and dying, their faces contorted in pain, or the blank look of death. Beams of heavenly light bathed them in a soft, comforting glow.

"That's gross, Lily," Renata said. "Where did you get that?"

Lily pointed to the small library room behind us, and then at the parting clouds on the page, from where the hand of God reached down to receive the fallen soldier.

Sign for?

"You're not supposed to look at stuff like that!" Renata snatched the book away. "It'll give you nightmares."

I still hadn't looked up the sign for heaven. I'd meant to, but I'd forgotten.

"I'm not sure, Lily." I demonstrated a sign that was a combination of *clouds* and *light*. "It's probably something like that."

My deaf friends, the ones I learned sign language from,

never talked about heaven, or hell, or God. We talked about boys and shopping and movies. I knew the signs for *make out, gossip,* and all the swears there were signs for, plus some that we'd made up, but God just never entered the conversation. Even though they told us at camp to go forth and spread the Good Word to any straying youth we knew, I was too chicken to try it on anyone but Teddy. He was already a believer anyway and probably didn't count because he was too mentally handicapped to stray much or mean any harm by it if he did.

Lily practised the made-up sign for heaven a couple of times.

"I'll look it up," I told her. Her family had the biggest sign language dictionary I'd ever seen. It sat on the coffee table in the living room. Lily's mom put it there so that it was available to everyone, but it was mostly her mom and me who used it.

Play family now, Lily signed. *You baby, me mommy.* She dragged me over to the little playhouse and sat me down and pulled out all the things to make pretend cookies.

As we popped the pretend cookies into the oven, I looked up. Hans was coming across the room, alone. I tried to stand up, hit my head on the playhouse ceiling, and reeled back, landing hard on my butt. He peered through the window and thankfully, mercifully, did not laugh. God was not only watching, He must've been in the room right beside me to work a miracle like that.

"Are you okay?"

"Yeah." I crawled out of the playhouse and stood up. "I was just trying to make Lily laugh."

Lily stared solemnly up at us, the pretend tray of cookies in her hands. She lifted it up. Hans took an invisible cookie, and so did I.

Go, I signed. *Leave us alone for just a minute, okay?*

Lily shook her head, offering the tray up again. Hans took another cookie.

"They're really good, Lil. Thanks."

Lily beamed.

"So, Della." He pretended to eat a cookie. "I know I shouldn't talk with my mouth full," he said, muffling his words. Lily laughed her strange, squeaky, breathless laugh. "I was wondering what the sign was for *pretty.*"

Now I, of all people, knew perfectly well that the world's biggest sign language dictionary was just sitting there, totally available, on the coffee table in their living room. There was no reason why he couldn't look it up when they got home, which would be a matter of minutes. He was one of the smartest guys in our class. Resources were not lost on him. He came first in the library scavenger hunt in the fall. I came in second, but that's not the point.

The point is that he was asking me about the sign for a reason.

"Pretty like, b-b-beautiful?" The word caught in my throat. "Or like *pretty* stupid?"

Lily set the tray down and opened her arms. Hans lifted her up and swung her onto his back.

Horse, she signed. *Fast!*

"Pretty like beautiful."

I showed him, the hand gesturing the sweeping beauty of someone's face. He repeated it, thanked me, and then galloped off, with Lily wheezing gleefully on his back.

Teddy came down with the flu that night, and then Hans and Renata and the dad and two of the older kids, who probably brought it home from bible college in the first place. Lily was fine for a few days, but then got it twice as bad. She was rushed to the hospital, feverish and short of breath. The infection had gone straight into her lungs, made all the more susceptible because the tracheotomy was a direct route for infection.

She was in the children's hospital in the city, so I had to wait for the weekend when my mom could drive me in for a visit. I went to the mall with all the money in my piggy bank and bought Lily a white plush elephant with silver wings and a card, even though she couldn't read. On Saturday morning I called the hospital to find out what room she was in.

"There's no one here by that name," the woman said.

"Are you sure? Lily Van Luven." I said it louder.

"I heard you, dear. There's no patient here by that name." There was a long pause. "Is there an adult there I can talk to?"

"Her name is Lily Van Luven! I know she's there."

"Sweetheart." My mother dried her hands. "Let me."

The woman on the phone sighed. "Is your mother there?"

"Maybe it's under Luven?"

"Let me, okay?" My mother took the phone. "Yes, I'm her mother." She put a hand on my shoulder as she listened.

"L-u-v-e-n!" My heart pounded. "Spell it for her!"

"I see. I understand. Yes, thank you. Goodbye." She hung up the phone. "They can't release any information about her. Sweetheart, sometimes that means — "

I ran for my room, slamming the door behind me. My mother was a nurse. She knew! She *knew* what it all meant.

I heard her phoning someone, talking briefly, and then hanging up. She knocked on my door. When I didn't answer, she came in anyway.

"She developed pneumonia." She sat on the edge of my bed and petted my hair. "Lily died this morning. I'm sorry, sweetheart."

Her coffin was a little white box, open, with her teddy bear and favourite toys and spring flowers piled around, even though she was allergic to flowers. The sermon was in English, but Lily's dad did the eulogy in German, after his English faltered. Hans and Renata and the others sang the adoption song in both English and German. My mom held my hand and cried and cried, even though she'd never met Lily or their family and had only come because she didn't think I should go to my first funeral alone. Then, the minister invited up anyone who wanted to speak, to say their goodbyes or bring forward any tokens they wanted to share. I joined the line, with the stuffed elephant and get-well card and a photocopy of the sign for heaven from my sign language dictionary.

It's true when they say dead people look asleep, only I know they glue their lips and eyelids shut and put make-up on and shampoo and blow-dry their hair. At the cemetery there was more talk about God's will, and the place He keeps for each one of us in heaven. At the reception, there was even more talk about God's will, and how it was Lily's time to "go with God." I sat on the steps and thought of all the ways I could get back at God for doing such a rotten thing. How dare He take her, after she was born so early and addicted to drugs, and then spent three years bopping from one crappy foster home to another. Then, just when she gets adopted by one of the sweetest, kindest families on the planet, wham! Bang! Pow! Enough of that happiness, better show those little people down there My Almighty Power. God was a cheater! Taking Lily was just plain cheating. The whole thing was a fraud!

I found my mom, who was weeping in the bathroom, and told her I wanted to go and would meet her at the car. As I left, I passed a table by the door, with a picture of Lily and all the things people had brought her. I'd thought she was going to be buried with all that stuff. That's why I'd photocopied the sign for heaven for her so she'd know it for when she got there.

If she got there. If there was a *there* to get to. After all, if God was a fraud, then what did that say about heaven? But then, what about Lily? What and *where* was she now? A pure soul floating above us, watching? Energy expelled into the atmosphere? A reincarnated being in some alternate universe? Limbo? Nothing? Nowhere? Just a rotting corpse? It was easier to believe that, as awful as it was, than to believe in some kind of fluffy, wonderful heaven. I squeezed my eyes shut, trying to get rid of the image of her in that coffin under the dirt, decomposing while I just went along with my life.

When I opened my eyes, I noticed a little stubby home-made book on the table that said *To Lily, Love Hans* on the front. It was one of those books you flip the pages of, and the drawings on each page form a rough animated cartoon. When I flipped the pages there was an image of hands sign-ing *pretty girl.* I looked around, made sure no one was watching, and then slipped it in my pocket and left.

In the car, my mother took my hands and gulped back a sob.

"Do you want to pray together?"

"No." I pulled away. "I fired God. If He even exists to be fired."

"Della . . . " She placed her hands on the steering wheel and took a deep breath, as if she might launch into a sermon about how it was impossible to fire God. Thankfully, mercifully, she didn't. We drove home in silence, and she let me stay in my room all afternoon, and even brought me supper and left it on a tray outside my door, and kept my brother quiet and out of the way.

A Few Words for
My Brother

ALISON LOHANS

. . .

Right now it hurts too much to talk about. I wish the numbness would come back. The feeling of unreality that lets you go around thinking maybe it didn't happen. Instead, there's this bleak . . . *nothing*. The impossible unfairness of it all. The total humiliation. Only words, all of this. What are words, anyhow? Just little bits of sounds and shapes that are supposed to mean something.

. . .

IN THE NEWSPAPER:

High Speed Chase Leads to Arrest of Youth, 15

Youth court justice Nancy Duczek sentenced a local youth, 15, to six months' confinement at the Willard Hoskins Centre on twenty-one charges.

The youth, a repeat offender, was apprehended last Tuesday following a high speed chase in a stolen vehicle.

The Chevrolet Blazer with Manitoba plates was first spotted at 2 a.m. heading east on Walker Avenue.

The male driver proceeded in an erratic fashion, colliding with several parked vehicles in the 36th Street lot of Reliable Used Autohaus before racing down Fortuna Avenue and south on Llewellyn Drive.

Police reported that the Blazer was clocked at speeds of up to 140 km on three separate occasions. The driver refused to pull over or stop when a roadblock was set up on 93rd Street.

The vehicle later plunged onto the CN track where it collided with a freight car. The Jaws of Life were required to remove the three occupants.

A male passenger, also 15, was hospitalized and is in highly critical condition. Charges are pending. A 13-year-old female, believed to be in the vehicle under duress, was hospitalized with injuries said to be non-life-threatening.

The driver has been charged with auto theft, driving under the influence of alcohol, driving without a licence, driving without due care and attention, and failure to stop for an officer of the law. Other charges include twelve counts of break-and-enter, possession of stolen goods, mischief over $5000, unlawful confinement, and possession of an illicit substance. The names of the youths have been withheld according to the provisions of the Youth Criminal Justice Act.

As if that will keep people from knowing!

. . .

ON TV:

Wrecked cars in a used car lot, dented big time. Big scrape on the side of a building. Smashed-up Chevy Blazer being hauled away from an orangey-brown train car. The windshield is spiderwebbed with shattered glass.

. . .

PORTRAIT ABOVE THE PIANO:
Three little kids aged seven, seven and five. Raine smiling, wispy blonde hair falling out of the blue barrette into her face even though Mom fussed with it in the studio. Devin acting goofy. Mouth pursed up in a puckery shape sort of like the knotted end of a balloon, eyes looking slantwise. Me with an innocent smile — but only because the photographer made me laugh all of a sudden. Devin kept pinching me. Hard. Always when Mom wasn't watching.

Mom was pregnant with me when Devin's adoption papers were signed. I used to feel really confused when people asked if he and I were twins. I knew Devin didn't grow inside Mom. "Twins of our hearts," Mom always told the people. I used to wonder how hearts could have twins.

. . .

Why didn't Devin get hurt? He hurts everybody else.

. . .

Words. What do I say to Tori? What can she say to me? She's always nice about it, but I know Devin gives her the willies.

She phoned afterwards. "How can you *stand* it?" she said.

"I can't," I said. My throat got tight and I started shaking, so I didn't talk much longer. With Dad going to the police station and then the lawyer's and youth court — plus going to work — *and* to Hoskins and the hospital, with Mom spending a lot of time at the hospital too, I'm on my own more than I like. Except, I don't want to be *with* anybody either.

I know Tori's nice, polite family is shocked. That they think there's something wrong with us. Maybe there is.

Tori's still on my side. I hope. "I know it's that fetal alcohol disorder," she's told me more than once.

. . .

Devin's earlobes aren't shaped right. His eyes are set far apart. His face is kind of flat.

His birth mom was a university student. One who partied a lot.

. . .

The ringing phone blasts through my entire nervous system.

"Hailey." It's Mom. "Have you had anything to eat?"

"I'm not hungry." I pace around with the cordless. Kick a Home Depot flyer that's lying in the middle of the living room rug. Most of the time I feel nauseated.

There's a sigh. "When did you eat last?"

"Breakfast." It's a lie.

There's so much silence I know Mom's trying to remember. "You have to eat." She doesn't say it with conviction — *conviction!* I could argue her down with just a word or two. I almost feel like trying. But that would be cruel.

"Whatever. I'll have an apple."

"Hailey." There are all kinds of things she can nag me about. Eating. Going to school. Even taking a shower. But her voice is pale and limp.

"*What?*"

Another sigh. I feel her withdrawing, pulling every scrap of energy back into that hard tight shell that walks around wearing my mother's clothes. Pulling back to the hospital, where Raine . . . I don't want to think about my sister. It's too —

"I *will* eat." My shoulder scrunches the phone against my ear so hard it hurts.

"Whatever."

Did my mother actually *say* that?! Before I can ask, the line clicks. I feel like throwing the stupid phone in the garbage. But that's a Devin-kind of thing and I'm not going anywhere near that place.

Mitzi gets in my way. I step over her but she whines and follows me, and I almost trip. "Mitzi!" I yell.

She cringes. Her ears flatten; her little stub of a tail wags submissively.

"Mitz . . . I'm sorry." I kneel. Hug her — lean against her, actually, and feel that cold nose and gentle tongue go to work on my cheek. But she's restless. A few licks, and then she's whining again. Does she need to go out? Did I feed her this morning?

The front door's closer than the dog dish. I notice that yellow leaves have fallen on the grass where Mitzi squats to pee. She barely misses the hose, which is stretched out like a confused green snake.

Devin deliberately stepped on her paw about two weeks ago. For no reason. His face suddenly got this evil look — and then he just *did* it. He didn't see me watching from the hall. After she yipped, he petted her until Mitzi slunk away. I slunk away too, filled with hate. For Devin, and for his ignorant, selfish birth mom.

I don't like going upstairs to my room. But I have to, sometimes. Raine's bed sits there by the wall. With the blue hummingbird comforter so smooth and the pillow placed so perfectly, it's like something in a furniture store display. My bed's a tangle of sheets. I look at it now, look at Raine's *Lord of the Rings* poster hanging by the desk. Raine wants to see New Zealand someday.

My throat seizes into a hurting knot. Then I'm on my sister's untouched bed, crying my guts out.

. . .

IN THE NEWSPAPER:

> FLYNN, ADEN ETHAN. Tragically on Oct. 20 at the tender age of 15. Our hearts are breaking dearest Son. Left to mourn your passing are Mother Deanna Davis, Step-Dad Jordan Hughes, Father Mick Flynn, brothers Zander, Ty, Blake & Lucas, sisters Emily & Karley, & Grandpa & Grandma. Services Oct. 25 at 2 p.m. at St. Peter's Church.

. . .

"We should go."

"I'm not having anything to do with those people."

"How do you think they feel about *us?* The least we could do is pay our respects."

In the kitchen Mom and Dad are throwing words at each other. Dad is a stiff board standing at the sink. A solid wall with no windows.

I look at the newspaper photo of Devin's dead friend. A cocky smile, with chin jutting forward, and hair down to his shoulders. In black-and-white the sneakiness doesn't show. The obituary doesn't tell about all that other stuff.

"Go if you like. I have better things to do with my time." Dad notices me. His jaw muscles are working. Like he's gritting his teeth on something that tastes awful.

"You are the most obstinate, self-centred — "

"Don't speak to me like that in front of our child."

Mom sags against the fridge. Sobbing, she looks so helpless I worry that she's going to keel over.

For a horrible moment all I hear is her choked cries. Plus Mitzi whining by the stove, and the clock ticking off every second. Then Dad goes to her, puts his arms around her. "I'm sorry, Jackie."

It's their own private drama. Once again I'm just the fly on the wall, and I turn to go. Suddenly, Mom is hugging me hard. "Thank God *you're* here, Hailey. And safe," she says into my hair.

I cling to her. But if I stay too long, I'll cry. Mom's tears make warm-then-cool splops on my neck. When I pull away, Dad leads her to the comfy chair in the living room.

I sit there on the floor, tracing the textured vinyl patterns with my fingertips. Mitzi comes to me; she snuffles my neck, then delicately licks. I hang onto her loving, furry self.

Does Devin know Aden died? Shivers race through my gut. How will he find out? Watching TV? From one of the guards? *Youth workers,* Dad calls them. Or, *staff.*

What will Devin do? What will they do to him if he flips out?

All of this is new and scary. Last time he was picked up he got three months' probation. That time wasn't as serious.

"Mom," I say loudly. "I'll go with you."

And then I'm so ashamed. Here I agree to go to Aden Flynn's funeral when I can't even make myself go to the hospital to see my own sister.

. . .

Aden Flynn. I've known him since kindergarten. Sometimes his clothes didn't fit right. Sometimes he didn't smell very clean. A squirmy kid who always got yelled at by teachers. And who was always having fights on the playground.

In class Devin never stayed in his desk. Sometimes he'd actually crawl around on the floor when the teacher was talking. He got yelled at a lot. There was the antisocial behaviour. Spitting. Scribbling on other people's assignments. Lying. Stealing. The bullying. Times like that, I'd pretend he wasn't my brother — just this jerk of a kid who happened to have the same last name as me. There's lots of Slaters in the phone book.

No wonder Devin gravitated to Aden. Aden accepted him. Nobody else wanted him around.

Who's to blame for all of this?

. . .

VIDEO OF THE FUNERAL:

A scattering of people occupy the pews. The front seats are empty, reserved for the family. The organ plays softly. At the last minute Mrs. Slater and her older daughter, Hailey, sign the register, then step into the chapel and sit near the back. Wan and uncomfortable, they are clearly estranged from the other mourners. Considering the age of the deceased, there are curiously few young people in attendance.

The organ notes swell; those in the congregation stand as pallbearers solemnly enter with the casket, followed by others in the immediate family. The mother, a bleached blonde wearing dramatic black and sunglasses, sniffs audibly. It almost appears that this is her moment of glory, cast in a leading role. Or is she possibly suffering an allergic reaction to the flowers adorning the coffin?

During the service Mrs. Slater covers her eyes; she seems oblivious to the platitudinous ramblings of the minister. The daughter's face is curiously hardened. She studies the stained glass windows, which cast shafts of blue, violet and red across those seated below, and winces occasionally at the pastor's remarks about the tragic loss of this fine, upstanding young man who was so well loved by all who knew him.

The singing is sparse, the service short, lacking the usual testimonials of family and friends. As the grieving family exits down the centre aisle under the respectful and sympathetic gaze of those present, the black-clad mother sees the two Slater women. The blonde's features contort; she lunges. "You killed my baby!" her voice shrills over the gentle strains of the organ. Astounded, others pull her back. The Slater girl says something, but her words are lost in the commotion.

. . .

E-MAIL:

hey, hail!! are you still there??? haven't seen you in ages. how's your sister? even my mom keeps asking. hope she's going to be ok, that's AWFUL, what happened.

we had this impossible test in bio, all the genus-species stuff. i got a 52% but please PLEEEEZZZ don't tell anybody, i'll absolutely die!!! hey — is anybody bringing you the assignments? i just now thought about that. probably your mom or dad is taking care of that for you

> write! call me! i miss you a LOT
> xxx ooo xxx ooo xxx LUV, tori aka taurus
> p.s. makayla has the sweetest little kitten

. . .

PRE-RECORDED VOICE MAIL:
"This message is from the Twin Rivers Public School Division. A child in your household, Hailey Slater, a Grade Ten student at Douglas Collegiate, was marked absent from school today. Please press the *Pound* key to confirm receipt of this message, and telephone the school at your earliest convenience."

. . .

I open my cello case. Sandra totally understands why I didn't come to the last two lessons. The same with Dennis at orchestra. But my parents say I have to start doing some of my regular things. The way they said it, the words all had capital letters. Especially the HAVE TO part.

When I sit down, Mitzi sighs and goes upstairs. Does my playing sound *that* bad? Maybe she just knows she won't get any attention till I'm done.

Raine's violin case is parked by the piano. It hasn't moved since . . . Not unless Mom moved it doing housework — but probably not, because fluffy clumps of dog hair are lying around on the carpet. My eyes get wet. She was practising just before . . . And I was talking to Tori in the chat room . . .

To keep from crying, I squeeze my mouth into a hard line and look at the scratches on my cello. They're not the kind of marks you get from accidentally bumping against the latches on the case. Or dropping the bow. Right there on the front of my cello is graffiti. Like what you see downtown.

I cry.

I feel stupid, crying in the practice chair. So I tune. The Brahms sonata I'm playing at the next recital is too calm for how I feel. The Bach allemande is too cheerful. *Kol Nidrei* is more like it, even though I've just started that song for lessons. I merge with its sorrowful mood as my fingers curve over the strings and my bow pulls the sounds out. Every now and then the piano strings hum along. After a while I'm in this huge bubble where the vibrations reach through to touch every part of me, and my body's swaying with the music. Then tears don't matter. Except, they make it harder to see the notes.

The end of the song is very peaceful.

When I'm done, the words start coming back. *Fetal Alcohol Syndrome. Stolen Blazer. Horrendous accident. Concussion. Face shredded by flying glass . . . Sentenced to six months . . .*

I look up at the three little kids in the portrait over the piano. Back then, who would've guessed this could happen?

There's a movement off to the side. Both Mom and Dad have been watching me.

"Hailey, that was beautiful," Dad says, and wipes his eyes. "Thank you very much."

I nod and look at Raine's violin. I think about the poster

on our bedroom wall, and how she wants to see New Zealand someday.

My eyes keep right on leaking.

. . .

School is terrifying. People quit talking anytime I come near. Nobody knows what to say. Tori's like a shepherd, guiding me everyplace she can. But we don't have all our classes together. Sometimes she talks to Makayla, and they'll laugh about something or other. Then she remembers, and feels guilty. Levi Watson keeps looking at me. As if he wants to say something but doesn't know how. Weird, how I forgot about him for all that time.

I'm behind in classes. Miss a couple of weeks, and it's like a different language. Especially Math. The teachers don't make it any easier. They *do* know what to say — or think so, anyhow.

"How is your sister doing?" Ms. Campbell asks when I stay after to get my missed assignments. Her husband has Raine in his Grade Eight class in the school across the street.

Times like this, I wish I'd made myself go see her at the hospital. Except . . . I look at the equations on the chalkboard. "Okay, I guess." Since Ms. Campbell's silence means she's waiting for more, I have to put words together. "She has a concussion. She's conscious and everything, but . . ." The rest catches in my throat. *Lacerated face. Eyes . . .* Everything blurs. I hunch my shoulders and grab the papers she's holding.

"Let me know if we can help in any way."

"Thanks." It comes out so muffled she probably doesn't hear me.

In Socials there are two empty desks — Aden's and Devin's. Mr. Kitahara doesn't ask about Devin, though. "I hear your sister's in pretty rough shape," he says sympathetically.

Right away my chin wobbles. *Fractured jaw . . . Possible irreversible blindness . . . both eyes . . .* "Yeah," I stammer, and run out the door without getting the assignments. I'm still in the washroom crying when the bell goes.

I skip noon hour choir and feel more normal for Bio. "If you ever need to talk, I'm here," Mrs. Strongeagle says. She seems so *present*, so kind, and calm that maybe I'll remember what she said. She doesn't ask nosy questions.

After a week of this I realize *nobody* has asked about Devin. Not once. And that makes me sad.

. . .

"Hailey." Mom catches me as I'm about to e-mail Tori.

I reach for the mouse, hoping to put her off. "Just a minute."

Mom takes the mouse from my hand. She's back at work, and she looks really, *really* tired. There are creases between her eyebrows that weren't there before. I'm positive there's more grey in her hair. "It's been almost a month now," she says. And I know I won't be sitting down at the computer for awhile.

Almost a *month?* I hate myself.

We go into the kitchen. The sink is full of dishes. There are bags of unpacked groceries on the counter. I start putting them away. The plastic makes little swishing sounds.

"Thank you." Mom sounds surprised. "That's not what I wanted to talk to you about, though."

After getting on my case about the ostrich syndrome — and I said going to Aden Flynn's funeral proves I'm not an ostrich — my parents have been expecting me to visit Raine. She's lonely and scared, and wishes I'd come.

"I know." I juggle a box of macaroni in my hands and feel so ashamed.

Unspoken words float between us. *Face healing gradually . . . Blindness . . . Rope burns on her wrists . . .*

Tori and I spent about three hours in the chat room that night. Mom and Dad were at a meeting. Raine was practising, and didn't want to. If I'd been paying more attention, could I have stopped her from walking over to the mall with Devin to pick up a DVD? How was I to know? That it would get later and later — and nobody would come home except Mom and Dad?

Mom's eyes connect with mine as if she knows what I'm thinking. I set the macaroni down and reach for the bag of oranges. Raine doesn't remember anything about that night. Probably that's a good thing.

"I'll go," I say. Then, surprising even myself — "But I'll go see Devin first."

Glistening wetness spills from my mother's eyes. I know then that even after all these years of having such a difficult child in the house, she still loves my brother. A lot. We fall into one another's arms.

. . .

SECURITY CAMERAS AT THE WILLARD HOSKINS YOUTH CENTRE:
The girl looks apprehensive as she goes through the first set of doors with her father. A few people come and go; you can tell which ones are youth workers because they're relaxed. At the front desk the father and daughter empty their pockets and place their belongings in a locker. When the warden buzzes open another set of doors, the two proceed along the institutional corridor. It is eerily silent, apart from the whistling of a kitchen worker. The next set of doors remains locked until someone comes along with a key. The girl is biting her lower lip as she walks into the unit. She looks around at tables and couches, a TV. A ping-pong table.

"Hailey!" A youth approaches and stares at the girl. His features aren't quite right. *"You came to see me?"* There is a precarious silence.

Slowly, the girl opens her arms to her brother.

Dear Family —

DONNA GAMACHE

. . .

Some days I used to think it would have been better if my mother had died. Then I would know why she was no longer in my life.

But that's not what happened. Instead, she left on what was supposed to be a two-week trip to "get away from everything" and "find herself again." She never came home.

The "everything" she got away from included my little brother Murray, our dad, "Big Mike" McCormick, and me, Melinda. The 3M's people often call us.

I was eight when Mom left but Murray was only four. As far as I can remember we were pretty normal kids. Why she had to get away from us, I don't know. And when I question

Dad, he says he doesn't want to discuss it. I guess it still hurts him, too.

It was five years ago that she left, and we've managed, though it hasn't been easy. Maybe Dad guessed from the start that Mom wasn't coming back, but he didn't tell us. For a long time Murray and I kept thinking she'd return any day now. We'd hurry home from school and burst in the back door, calling her name. Or the telephone would ring and I'd run to answer it, sure that it would be Mom. Eventually we realized it wasn't going to happen.

Even now, there are days when I'll turn a corner at the mall and I'll think, for a minute, that the tall, blonde woman ahead of me is Mom. There are nights when I'll wake up dreaming of her, and she'll be laughing and we'll be singing together, just like when I was little.

For Dad, it's different now. He has a new girlfriend, Pauline, and they're talking marriage in the spring. Murray is starting to think of her as a mother. He doesn't really remember Mom, so it's easier to accept someone else. Me, I still remember.

The place where Mom "found herself again" was out in the mountains of British Columbia. At first she hooked up with a community of artists, kind of like a commune where they all lived together and shared the work, Dad said. She'd always been keen on painting, and she got into it really big there. Then after a few months she got her own place, a cabin in the mountains, and that's where she's spent her summers ever since. Winters, she goes down into Vancouver, rents an apartment, and finds a job of some sort. Then, come summer, she's back in the mountains, painting.

In the beginning she wrote every month or two. Then the spaces between letters got longer, and last year I think we heard from her twice. She never gives us an address, just a box number to write to. And she never writes to us individually, just one letter to everyone. "Dear family," she begins.

Our letters back have changed, too. At first we all wrote, with Dad helping Murray, but now I'm the only one. Why I bother, I don't know. She never answers my "When are you coming home?" or any of my other questions.

Last summer, finally, after he got serious about Pauline, Dad started divorce proceedings. That seemed to put an end to things for him. But not for me — which is why I decided that I had to see Mom again.

At first Dad was against it. "Your mother has never suggested it," he said. "She wants to be alone, and that's the way we'll leave her."

But I kept pushing, and eventually he realized how important it was to me. "If you have to go," he said, "it had better be in winter when she's down in Vancouver."

So I wrote to Mom at the end of November, and again in December and again in January, and now, February, it's happening. Mom agreed that I could visit her for three days. Dad put me on the plane, and I flew through two time zones, arriving just after noon, Vancouver time.

"I'll meet you at the airport," she'd written, but when I get off the plane there's an announcement for Melinda McCormick to come to the info desk, and there's a message from Mom saying I should take a taxi to her apartment. I'm still feeling nervous enough from flying alone without having to deal with a taxi, too, but there's no choice.

Wind is slashing rain against the window as the driver races his car through traffic. I watch out the window, my stomach a tight ball, and wish I hadn't come.

The taxi stops in front of a small, dreary-looking building, flat-topped, sided with dull grey bricks. I pay the driver, grab my suitcase and make a dash for the door. If this is winter in Vancouver, I'll stick to Winnipeg.

I skim over the list of tenants inside the door, and panic; there's no McCormick. Then I read the list more slowly and the K. Lucciana sinks in; Katrina Lucciana was my mother's maiden name. I start breathing again, and climb the stairs to apartment 203.

The door opens before I can ring the bell, like she's been standing there waiting for me. Her arms reach out, but I push past her into the room. Does she think I'm still an eight-year-old looking for a hug? I plunk down my suitcase and stare at her.

My mother looks younger than ever. Her hair used to be short, carefully styled each week at the hairdresser. Now it's longer than mine and straight, blonder than ever, with eyebrow-length bangs on her forehead. I'd remembered her as tall and a little bit plump — she was always dieting — but this woman is positively skinny, and her eyes are big beneath the long bangs.

She's looking me over, too. "I'd never have known you," she says abruptly.

"It's been a long time." All the hurt I've felt at five years' desertion is in the words.

She blinks and looks away. "Sorry I couldn't meet you. I was going to borrow my neighbour's car, but it wouldn't start. Then I called for a taxi but there was more than an hour wait."

"It's okay," I say. My voice is stiff, like the rest of me. All the things I've saved up to say seem to have taken wing.

She moves my suitcase over beside a green plaid chesterfield. The room is small, the furniture shabby. A smell of oils or varnish permeates the air.

"I hope the smell of paint won't bother you," my mother says. "I don't usually paint here, but last night I did. You can sleep in the bedroom and shut your door against it."

"It won't bother me." We look awkwardly at each other, and then I try again. "Do you paint a lot?"

She shrugs. "Not in the winter. But I've a show starting. We've been hanging the pictures, and Manuel at the gallery wants a couple more." She motions towards the kitchen. "They're in there."

There are two large canvasses in the kitchen, each of them at least 50 by 70 centimetres. The one on the wall is of giant tulips in brilliant pinks and reds, against a background of bright green grass. The other is leaning against the wall. It's much darker — a water lily in palest yellow against dark, aquamarine water. The water drops on the petals are so real I'm sure they're still wet.

"The lily's not finished yet," Mom says, and turns it to face the wall. "Don't look at it closely till it's done."

I go over to examine the tulip picture close up. I'm impressed. I've studied art at school but nothing like this. The flowers seem to leap out of the background. It's almost as if I could reach out and pick one. I didn't expect her paintings to be so vibrant. The one at home of Murray and me is a small, pale watercolour.

"They're good!" I breathe. "Do you sell them?"

"Of course. That's how I make a living."

"Do you always paint so large?"

"Usually."

"Can I see the rest?"

"Later," she says. "Right now I need some food. What about you? Hungry?"

"I ate on the plane."

She moves restlessly around the kitchen, plugging in the kettle, putting bread in the toaster, eating a banana at the same time.

I sit on a stool beside the counter and watch her. She asks about my flight and my first impression of Vancouver. She doesn't ask about Dad or Murray.

When she's finished, she announces that we're going out

for groceries. "After that I'll start showing you Vancouver," she says. Digging into a small closet, she brings out a yellow raincoat. "You'll need this." I slip it on, ready for whatever comes.

The three days slip by. Mom treats me like a tourist. We visit Stanley Park and the aquarium, in the rain; Chinatown, in the rain; the Fraser River and the waterfront — still raining! It's like she's determined to show me a good time but to avoid any real conversation with me. At night, when I try to ask her questions about the past, she avoids answering or starts talking about Vancouver or her cabin in the mountains.

"I want to see the rest of your paintings," I remind her on my last afternoon. She nods and we take the bus to the gallery. Mom brings the tulip picture, but the water lily one isn't finished yet. She hasn't touched it since I came.

The gallery is on the second floor of a brown brick building. The stairs are narrow and dark, but the top floor is full of windows. Mom's art covers the walls, large canvasses of giant, multi-coloured flowers, larger than life-size, in fluorescent yellows and reds and pinks. Here and there she's added birds — parrots and other tropical ones — in bright reds and blues. It's like coming into a jungle. I almost expect to smell the flowers and hear the birds.

"These are all yours?" I ask in a whisper, though we're the only visitors.

She nods. "They're mostly from last summer, some from the year before. Look around. I need to show this to Manuel.

He does my framing." She takes the tulip painting over to the short, dark-skinned man who's working at the back.

I study her work. Besides the flowers and birds, there are a few of scenery — mountains and rivers in bold colours. But there are no city scenes, and none with people.

Mom comes over and starts explaining things about oils and acrylics, a lot of stuff I don't understand. I have a different question.

"Don't you paint people?" I break in. "I remember you painted Murray and me once." I don't tell her that the picture is still hanging in my room.

She stops talking, bites her lip and then shakes her head. "I never paint people now. Not since I came here." Abruptly, as though she's suddenly remembered something, she goes back to talk to Manuel.

I wander around for a few more minutes till Mom beckons me, and we leave. She seems in a hurry, but there's an ice cream shop nearby, and I practically drag her into it.

"My treat," I say, and without asking what she wants I order two strawberry sundaes, the kind we used to have — she and Dad, and Murray and I, all of us. We sit at the back and I think of all the questions I need to ask her.

"Why don't you paint people?" I ask instead.

She looks at her sundae, at the rest of the restaurant, and then finally at me. "You used to paint *us,*" I persist.

"I cut myself off from people when I came out here," she says finally.

"Why did you do that?"

She sighs. "I don't know. It just seemed necessary."

"Why did you leave? Why did you never come back?"

She hesitates. "I left because I had to."

"Why? What did Murray and I, or Dad, do to make you leave?"

She stares at me. "Oh, Melinda, you didn't *do* anything to make me leave. Surely you know that. I left because I felt like I was choking to death. I'd barely done any painting for years. I couldn't even bring myself to try."

"Because of time? Or money? Or what?"

"Time, a little bit, but not really. And not money. Your dad would have given me money for canvasses and paint, but he never understood. He thought I was wasting my time; he thought it was just a hobby."

For a minute we concentrate on our sundaes. Then she continues. "I never belonged, you know, to the life your dad wanted. We should never have married. We were too different. The rest of you — you were 'the three M's' and I was the odd one. I just couldn't fit in. I felt stifled, overwhelmed. I had to get out."

"You didn't love us?"

"I loved you. I still do. But I can't live with you. I need to live alone. That's what I realized after I came out here. And I need you to understand that, Melinda." She hesitates. "I'm glad you came to visit, though. You can come again if you want."

After that, I don't really seem to have any more questions. It's a long walk back to her apartment, and on the way she finally asks me about Murray, but not Dad, and I don't mention him or Pauline. I don't really understand my mother, but I want to try. Whether I'll come again, I'm not sure.

I've been using Mom's bedroom — she insisted — and I straighten it up and get my suitcase ready to leave.

"I'm going to bed early," I tell Mom after dinner. "I'll lose a couple of hours on the plane going back."

"Sure," she agrees. "I might do some painting. So if the light is on late, that's why."

It takes me a long time to fall asleep and the light is on all that time. I wake once, after midnight, and there's still a bright crack beneath my door.

In the morning I wake to silence. I open the bedroom door quietly. Mom is asleep on the chesterfield, her face young, her hair spread out around her.

I slip past her into the kitchen and switch on the light. The water lily painting is leaning against the stove. The water and the background in the picture are still dark and the overall effect is of darkness, but there's one main difference. In the lower right corner, something has been added. A young girl, maybe ten, maybe twelve, stands at the edge of the pond. She's wearing blue jeans and a denim shirt, so that she nearly fades into the background, but she's definitely there. Her arms are reaching out towards the lily as though she wants to pick it, or hold it. Somehow, the lily looks — I know it's strange — but somehow the lily looks willing, even eager to be picked.

"It's finished now," Mom says from behind me. "It's for you. I can send it once the show is over. If you want it."

"Oh, yes," I murmur, turning to give her a hug. "I want it."

I still don't understand her. I know we haven't solved things. But it's a start. The picture is a start.

Dreams in a Pizza Box

LIBBY KENNEDY

. . .

I can still see our home — our apartment with its thread-
bare nubbly gold carpet, trails and pathways etched
through rooms, the curled vinyl wallpaper tempting kids to
pick and peel, leaving a furry film on the walls. And the per-
petual smell of cat pee, though we never had a cat. I remember an angry knock at the door and an angrier voice
telling us to get out. Ma was crying, scared and mad at the
same time. She grabbed what she could, scooped my little
sister under her arm and pushed me out the door. She
turned back in one fluid sweep to grab an old pizza box that
sat on top of the fridge. I hadn't noticed the box until that
moment; it had always been there, as if it were part of the

refrigerator. With my sister under one arm, the pizza box dangling from her hand and me clenched to her other arm, Ma tried to be cheerful. She smiled and gave me a wink. She nibbled my sister's neck as we made our final exit down the worn-out wooden stairs. The etched glass door gave a parting moan then slammed rudely shut behind us. A slow teasing click — we were locked out. I looked back up to the two windows that had been ours. All I had were the memories of my sister and me inside the apartment, two innocent little faces steaming the windows and then our fingers drawing smiley faces in the condensation of warm macaroni and cheese breath. We climbed into our car and drove away.

I can vividly remember the first night in the car. It was exciting. Much like camping I thought. I'd never been camping. There was a scratchy plaid blanket in the car, and my favourite pillow, stained with yellowy drool circles. We drove around until it became dark then pulled into a deserted alley behind a strip mall, away from the glaring lights. Mom tucked us under the blanket. We asked for a bedtime story. Instead of the usual story, she pulled out the pizza box and showed us the contents, holding the bits and pieces high up to use the sliver of light that crept over the building. The box was crammed full of things she had collected over the years, treasures that she cherished. There were pictures cut from glossy fashion magazines of women with dark curls, silky olive skin and almond-shaped eyes wearing black dresses with big white polka dots. The models posed with Mona Lisa smiles, white-gloved hands placed on their narrow waists. There were *National Geographic* snippets, photographs of villages piled high along Mediterranean cliffs, whitewashed houses plastered together and topped with red brick roofs. The box contained some restaurant napkins and recipe cards with fancy swirled writing, a wine bottle cork, poems she had written, half melted candles: Italy, stuffed into a pizza box. She said we had family in Italy, relatives. One day soon we would go there. I dreamed of marble palaces that night, a city filled with alabaster towers and carved fountains, buildings glowing under an exotic distant moon, castles reflected in the shimmer of gentle waves. There was not a single door on the buildings in my dream city.

Weeks passed and the car filled with anything Ma could get her hands on. She refused to throw anything away in case we might need it one day. We collected wrappers, napkins and Styrofoam packaging from fast food restaurants. And used pizza boxes, tons of sticky, cheese-stained pizza boxes. We knew how to collapse the boxes to save space inside our car.

When my sister and I got hungry we had to search for our food. We went to the food bank to see what they had. We couldn't use most of the food they gave us; we didn't have a can opener, didn't have a pot or stove to cook macaroni. Once all they gave us was a huge head of cabbage and some mushy brown bananas. We went to lots of restaurants, but we didn't actually buy food there. Ma picked through the trash bins behind fast food restaurants looking for left-overs that others tossed out or even half-empty plastic drink cups with their lids still on. We felt lucky when we found partially eaten hamburgers and maybe some cold fries covered in grease and salt. Sometimes we even found spongy syrup-drenched pancakes. We ate packets of sugar. And ketchup. Ma would pull the little foil packages open and we would suck out the tangy ketchup. Or she would make tomato soup by mixing the ketchup with warm water that she brought from the washroom sink in the restaurants. We drank warm dairy creamers and cola diluted with melted ice. Behind the grocery store in a big blue dumpster Ma often found fruit and vegetables. All we had to do was pick through the squishy rotten bits. The bakery tossed out mouldy loaves of bread. Since I didn't like the crusts anyway, we would pull off the fuzzy green crusts and eat the middle of the loaves. The food we ate was usually cold and often it smelled terrible. But I never complained to Ma; she tried so hard to keep us fed. I was always hungry, always had a growling knot in the pit of my belly. I can only imagine that Ma felt the same pangs of hunger because she gave my sister and me most of the food she found.

Periodically there was a knock on the window, and we were told to move the car. We had overstayed our welcome, Mom said, but I'm not so sure that was the case — I don't think we were welcomed in the first place. The car ran, but we had to conserve gas. We kept finding secret new places to park. A new adventure every few days.

Then one day a cop told us to move and we couldn't. The car wouldn't start. He called a tow truck. The officer let us grab what we could, some clothes, our blanket, and my pillow. Ma grabbed a photo of the Leaning Tower of Pisa from the dash and crammed it back into the pizza box. I tried to take some of the empty pizza boxes we had collected but Ma told me we'd get some new ones. We watched our home roll away.

That night we walked for hours. My sister was old enough to walk, but for the most part Mom carried her. My sister had her pink wrinkled thumb stuck in her mouth and her head resting on Ma's shoulder. I wanted badly to hold Ma's hand but she already had her hands full. I was too old for that anyway. We found a stairwell behind an old movie theatre that showed foreign films and we curled up there to sleep. The sound of passionate foreign voices and the serenade of violins and musky operatic songs seeping through the door of the theatre comforted me. Mom held us in her arms and kissed our foreheads over and over. I can still remember her saying, "It'll be all right, we'll be fine. You'll see." Then it rained. I missed the car. At least in the car we were protected from the wind and rain. When we lived in the car the seats had been comfortable and we could lock the doors to feel safe.

That night the rain came in frozen sheets, drenching our

blanket with ice water. We moved and found shelter behind another building, a dark doorway to a fancy Italian restaurant. But the owner told us to get lost. I didn't want to leave. I love the smell of cooking garlic. I could imagine myself slurping up foot-long strands of spaghetti drenched in rich, chunky tomato sauce. As we moved away, Ma pretended to speak Italian to us. "*Mi Amore,*" she'd say, kissing our cheeks as we journeyed down endless sleet-soaked alleyways. At that moment we were in Venice, gliding along mysterious canals.

Soon after we left the Italian restaurant Ma got sick. She said it hurt when she coughed; she shivered even though I thought she felt like she was on fire when I touched her. For several days we moved around the city, slept where we could, in the park, on the beach between driftwood logs and even under a pedestrian overpass. We couldn't find a warm place to sleep, couldn't dry ourselves. When Ma thought I was asleep she would cry quietly.

Someone at the food bank told us to go to the women's shelter. They would have beds for us, maybe some clean clothes and dry blankets. We were excited, filled with hope. Maybe this was a sign of better things for us. When we reached the shelter it was full. With winter coming, many other women and children had moved in from alleys, from stairwells and underground parking lots. Ma begged them to take my sister and me and promised that she would come back for us. She gave us each a kiss and then left us, left her pizza box stuffed with dreams. She never came back.

I don't remember exactly where our old apartment was but I imagine it looks much like the one we live in now. With help from the women's centre and our foster parents my sister and I went to school. After graduation they helped us find jobs and this apartment. We now have a home and I feel like we are a family again. Less one. Our apartment is small, situated above an alfresco cafe. By noon each day the air around us is filled with the pungent aroma of roasting garlic. I am sure Heaven must smell like this. There are two windows that face the street below. Between the windows I have several tiny framed pictures. My little piece of Italy strategically placed on the wall, a shrine to the memory of Ma.

For years we searched for her. We searched shelters and alleys, looking in parked cars. Every time I see a discarded pizza box, I open it, hoping that it might be hers, filled once again with her dreams.

Hang On

PATRICIA McCOWAN

. . .

When Randy's mom opened their front door I could tell she'd been crying. Before I could say anything, she grabbed my arm, kind of strong, and said, "Well hi there, Kevin. We've missed you. Come on in," and pulled me inside. "I was just making a snack for Mr. Krawchuk and me. Come on into the kitchen."

Though I wasn't hungry I couldn't say no when Mrs. Krawchuk looked so sad but sounded so cheerful.

The house was quieter than usual, and it didn't smell like it always does, of cookies or pies or Mrs. Krawchuk's famous cinnamon loaf.

In the kitchen, Mr. Krawchuk was leaning against the

counter with his arms crossed, staring at the floor. He has the hairiest arms of any dad I know and they're really big, too, so when he crosses them they look like cartoon arms, like Brutus in Popeye.

He looked up and smiled at me like of course I should be coming over for a snack while Randy is in a coma. He unfolded those Brutus arms and put his hand on my shoulder, giving it a big squeeze. I nodded, waiting for him to say something — something about Randy or maybe even about the snack Mrs. Krawchuk was making, but he just stood there squeezing my shoulder. When it started to hurt and I felt stupid nodding, he let go and left the kitchen without saying anything.

Mrs. Krawchuk was busy cutting up some marble cheese and piling it on a plate. The cat clock above the kitchen table ticked, its eyes and tail clicking back and forth with each second. It had been more than a week since the accident and my mom said it would be okay to see Randy's parents.

I knew I should say how sorry I was about what happened or ask how they were, but I couldn't. I've never been in the Krawchuk's kitchen without Randy before. He always does the talking. He jokes with his dad or mimics his mom until she says something like, "That Mrs. Krawchuk sure is gorgeous," and Randy goes, "Ugh, okay, okay, I'll stop."

It's great being with them when they laugh. I never have to say anything. Usually.

"So, um. How's Randy?"

"So, you know, we visited the hospital this morning — "

"Hey, Kevin," Randy's dad was suddenly back in the kitchen. "Have you seen our latest painting?"

"Uh, I don't think so."

"Oh, it's lovely," Mrs. Krawchuk piped in, sounding relieved. "Go ahead, Kevin, have a look. I promise to save some cheese and crackers for you," she added, as if there were a risk she might devour them all while I was out of the room. She kept fussing with the plate and didn't turn to face me.

I was starting to feel as though I was in one of those dreams where everyone looks like themselves but says stuff that makes no sense and you have to go along with it because it's a dream and you can't help it. They're not as scary as nightmares but they feel almost worse, like your arms will fall off and everyone in the dream will keep talking as if nothing's happening.

I followed Mr. Krawchuk into their living room. He put his hands in his pants pockets and stopped in front of the piano. Randy's taken piano lessons since he was little and he's really good at it for a normal, fun person. He plays it like he rides his bike — fast and entertaining. The piano was closed but Randy's lesson book was still open on it, as if he'd just left. The new painting was above the piano.

The painting was mainly blue and showed an old-fashioned ship with sails in some moonlit harbour. There was a moonlit hill with moonlit old buildings on it behind the moonlit ship. The moon was reflected in the moonlit water.

A little gold sign on the bottom of the painting's curlicue frame had "Moonlight — M. Bolivar" engraved on it.

Mr. Krawchuk's hand was back on my shoulder. He stood behind me. "Mrs. Krawchuk and I love our landscape paintings. Every year we like to pick one up at that fine art sale out at the Holiday Inn by the airport. Makes sense to buy landscapes by the airport, eh? It's like every painting is a little trip abroad. This new one's Spanish, I'm pretty sure. And we've got that Venetian one over the couch, all those gondolas, there. And the English moor with that nice castle ruin, above the buffet. Randy hasn't seen this new one yet, but I bet he'll like it, don't you? His mom and I bought it and put it up here when you boys were out, ah, riding out there . . ." Mr. Krawchuk took his hand off my shoulder and covered his face. He didn't finish his sentence.

Mrs. Krawchuk had come into the living room with the plate of cheese in one hand and some little square napkins in the other, and when she saw Mr. Krawchuk she said, "Oh, Len," and put everything down on the coffee table and went over and put her arms around him. They stood there crying and hugging in the middle of their living room in front of me. I wished I could disappear.

I stared hard at "Moonlight" and tried to swallow down the fat ball of sadness that lurched up into my throat. But I didn't really want to look at harbours or gondolas or ruins. I wanted to be with Randy again.

Like I had been the day Randy showed up on his bike.

I shiver by my back door. "Aren't you supposed to be practising?" I'm still in my pyjamas, it's drizzling and cold out. A boring kind of day.

"Ah, I can skip a Saturday. I know the stuff backwards. Besides, my mom and dad are out."

We ride around on our bikes. The school yard, the Seven-Eleven. We do wheelies in the big empty parking lot of the closed-down grocery store. No one's around. So we go further, to the tracks past the candy factory, where the air smells like licorice allsorts, even in the drizzle. We like to ride over the tracks, we like the bumps. We give each other little challenges, to make things interesting. Who can get over the fastest? Who can do it with their eyes closed? Randy usually wins.

"*Who can take a sunrise, sprinkle it with poo, fart it out his butt and make a miracle or two? The Candy Man. The Candy Man can.*" Randy sings loudly, his voice wavering as he bounces up and over the rail crossing to the other side of the tracks. "Your turn," he calls across to me.

I'm laughing. "I don't want to sing. I'll just ride. I can't think up — "

"Come on, it's funny. I'll start you. '*Who can take some french fries . . .*'"

It's hard to say no to Randy. I pedal my bike up the embankment to the crossing and sing, off-key as always, "*Sprinkle them with glue, get them stuck together so . . .* um . . . oh, crap." When I come down the hill my bike hits a puddle and I feel water shoot up my back.

Randy laughs beside me. "Nice rhyme, Kev. Glue and crap. *Unique.*"

Unique is Randy's favourite word for anything he thinks is stupid or gross or funny. He pronounces it like it's foreign — youneekwee.

"Yeah, yeah," I say, twisting on my bike to see how dirty my pants are. I hear the rumble of a train coming, but I'm trying to wipe the wet mud off my jeans with the sleeve of my jacket. Mom yells at me when the laundry's really dirty. "It's too wet out here, let's head back." I turn to face Randy again and he's leaning over his handle bars, facing away from me, looking down the tracks.

"Hang on," he says.

I think he means wait until we can cross again. He sits up and puts his right foot on the pedal. There are no crossing bars that come down to block our way, I guess because this crossing isn't used much anymore. People are just supposed to look.

The train's coming closer, its light shines down the line toward us through the rain.

Randy's humming something I can't make out. The train sounds its horn, two short, loud blasts. It's seen us.

I feel very happy right then. I'm on my bike beside Randy, waiting for the wind and rattle of a train passing in front of us, thinking of going back to his house for something to eat. We'll get out of the rain and read comics.

The train's so close I feel the ground vibrating up through my bike. If Randy and I were younger we'd try throwing a penny on the track right now to see what it would do. But we don't throw pennies anymore.

"Hey, Randy, remember the pennies — "

"Now!" Randy yells. He stands on his pedals. He lowers his head. I can hear he's singing something but the sound of the train's horn fills the air around me. My mouth opens and all I hear is the train.

He's up the embankment, he's on the track, the train's light flares over him like a spotlight. The train smashes his back wheel. A wall of flashing steel is in front of me, blocking out everything. My blood pounds through my whole body as the train goes by.

Did he make it? Did he make it? Did he make it?

"The doctors don't know if he's going to make it. They can't say, yet." Mrs. Krawchuk was wiping her eyes and then drying her fingers on her apron. Her mouth smiled but her eyes stayed sad. "All we can do is hope."

Mr. Krawchuk fisted his tears away and coughed harshly a few times. "Well, now," he said, but he had to cough again. "Well, now, let's have this little snack together, shall we? Make us all feel better. Randy would want us to."

So we sat down and forced the cheese and crackers dry down our throats for Randy. They said they'd take me with them back to the hospital to visit Randy that afternoon if my mom said it was okay. I said she would and they said they'd phone her to make sure.

I looked up at "Moonlight" again and decided I hated it. The empty ship that would never leave the harbour. The buildings that would always be dark. The moon that would never make way for the sun.

Mr. Krawchuk noticed me staring. "You think Randy'll like it?" he asked.

I swallowed down the last cracker I could manage. "He'll say it's unique." I said it the proper way for Mr. Krawchuk. Not Randy's way.

He smiled and nodded. "Unique," he repeated.

I almost laughed. For Randy.

Balance Restored

JESSIE MAY KELLER

. . .

DENIAL

A soft breeze wafts through the open window and wakes me. I sniff the air. Magnolia blossoms. Today Jake and I will bicycle to the lake. We'll take our bathing suits and I'll make sandwiches. He loves cheese and ham. Tomatoes and lettuce for me (I'm a vegetarian). We'll pick up something to drink on the way. With my eyes still shut, I turn my pillow over, plump it up. It feels damp. Maybe I'll take just another half hour.

"Alexandra. Alexandra!" I catch Mom's perfume (Opium) as she shakes my shoulder. I don't want to get up.

"Go away. I need to sleep." I scrunch up and bury my head in the blankets.

"Honey, you really must get up. You've just got time to dress. We have to be at the chapel at nine."

At the chapel? Dress? But Jake and I are going . . . I hear the screech of brakes. I see the truck directly in front of us. I feel the impact as the air bag hits me. I scream and scream and Jake isn't moving and the horn is honking and honking and blood gushes out of his mouth and I see lights flash. My body slowly slides into a long, dark tunnel.

I'm in the chapel. It's unreal. There are so many flowers: magnolias, tulips and daffodils. People cry and hug each other. The minister talks. I'm not going to listen. I'll escape to some place warm. I'll pretend I'm at the lake. Jake and I will lie on the sand and let the sun bake us. We'll see who gives in first and makes a mad dash for the water. I can feel it now — icy cool, like plunging into melted popsicles. The colour orange. Amber really. We met at school, at the vending machine. I turned away, an orange popsicle in my mouth, when a hand touched my shoulder and a laughing voice said, "Hey! My favourite. I hope you left one for me." Jake loved popsicles. He loved the lake. We float in the amber liquid. Cool, refreshing. Jake holds my hand.

ANGER

I'm really mad at you, Jake. Really pissed off. You promised me so many things. We had plans. What about UBC next year? Do I go by myself? You know I get lost easily. How will I find my way around the campus without you? Did you think

*about that? Who will help me with math? We had an agree-
ment. I would check all your English papers, you would be my
math tutor. It's not fair. I hate this.*

Everything looks black now. I have this tight feeling in
my chest. Tonight at dinner my brother David was late. He
raced down the stairs, crashed into my chair and milk
spilled all over the table. "You stupid idiot," I yelled. "Can't
you see where you're going? Do you always have to wreck
everything?" Now I'm upstairs, staring at my homework.
The words all blur together. They don't make sense. Nothing
makes sense. I'm going for a bike ride.

I get my Nishiki out of the garage. As I coast down the
back lane, I'm swamped by the heavy scent of magnolias. I
crouch low over the handlebars, turn onto Front Street and
peddle fast and hard. The warm air whips my long hair
against my face. The pain is comforting. A few kids are playing pick-up in the park. I race by the elementary school,
grind up the hill toward the library, wheel around and head
for the river. I sit by the dark water for a long time. Birds
rustle in the aspens. A big moon rises in the sky. I see its
reflection in the water. The chunk of ice in my chest throbs.
My mouth is dry and bitter-tasting. I stand, grab stones and
hurl them at the water. The moon's image breaks up, scat-
ters. Suddenly my stomach turns. I retch violently. Great
spasms rip through my gut. The pain recedes. I scrunch
down, cup water in my hands and splash it onto my face
and head. Slowly, I make my way back home.

BARGAINING

Okay, God, I promise things will be different. Honest. No lies to Mom and Dad, hey, no lies, period. I'm definitely going to be on the straight and narrow. No more drinking. I'll go to church every Sunday. I'll join the choir. I'll volunteer to help with the Day Care. I'm going to be good to David. I know he's just a kid. He tries really hard to be good to me. I'll go out of my way to talk to him. I'll let him sit on my bed. I'll listen to him practise his guitar. I'll help him with his homework. Honestly God, if you make my life okay again, really okay, I promise, cross my heart and hope to die, I promise things will be different.

I'm in my bedroom, on my knees. On my knees for God's sake. I hurt so badly. I just want everything to go back to April 19th. I want my life back. It was a good life. Jake and I were so good together. Everybody said so. I don't understand why it happened. I try and try to understand. I wake up each morning and I smell the magnolias and I hear Mom in the kitchen downstairs and I think, *Hey, this is going to be a great day.* And then it hits me. It's not going to be a great day. It's going to be another shitty day. *I miss you Jake. I want you back. I want to talk to you. I want you.*

DEPRESSION

I wake up this morning and feel that I'm wrapped in a grey fog. I know I have a math exam at ten, my books are lying open beside me. But my legs won't move. I try to swing them over the edge of the bed but nothing happens. I lie here like a great grey sloth. My pajamas are too tight. My skin is hot and sticky. No scent of magnolias drifts through the window. Just a cold, grey November morning. Rain raps at the window. Far, far away I hear voices — Mom, Dad and David. I hear the high hiss of the kettle. I hear Gus bark. I can't move. I don't want to move. I'm going to stay here forever. I don't want to go downstairs. I don't want to do my hair. I don't want a shower. I don't want to see the looks on their faces. I want to sleep. I need to sleep. I need to sleep for a century or two. Maybe more.

I've been thinking a lot lately. I should have seen the signs. I should have known something bad was going to happen. I should have done something to change things. What if I hadn't pushed Jake to go to the dance? What if we had gone to the movie instead? Why did I always make the decisions? I don't want to make decisions now. I don't care. I just want to sleep. I heard our song on the radio yesterday and I cried. I couldn't stop. Mom says it's normal. I know she's worried about me. I see her exchange looks with Dad and I can't deal with it. I just want to be by myself. Josie and Cara don't call much anymore. I don't blame them.

Jake, remember when we talked once about who would die first? Remember, I said it had to be me because I couldn't live without you? We decided we would die together when we were very, very old — about ninety. We had a list of all the things we were going to do first: a bicycle tour in southern France, a camel trip in Morocco, scuba diving, sky diving. We'll never take that first jump together, Jake. I'm crying again. Nothing's changed, Jake. I don't want to live without you. It's hard. It's too hard!

ACCEPTANCE

I laughed this morning. David told a stupid joke and I laughed and I saw tears in Mom's eyes and we were all laughing and David looked around sort of bewildered but thinking he'd done something brilliant. I gave him a hug and that confused him even more. Somehow it helped. The eggs and toast tasted good. Everything was fine until I sat down in the school cafeteria, opened my lunch and almost bit into a cheese and ham sandwich. I guess I had picked up David's lunch. Suddenly, I was back at the lake. I could feel the sun on my face. I could hear Jake's voice exclaiming as he opened the picnic basket. Gasping for breath, I ran from the lunchroom. Josie and Cara caught up to me in the hall and one on each side dragged me to the counsellor's office.

Mrs. Parker, the school counsellor, told me about the support group. At first it sounded like a dumb idea. The last thing I wanted to do was talk about Jake. But my group is pretty special. There are six of us. Somehow I find it easier to talk to these people. They all had someone die and they understand no matter what I tell them.

Today, Sara threw her journal at Maggie, the counsellor. It all happened so quickly. One minute Sara is curled up in her chair, the next, she's in the middle of the room and the book is flying. Maggie ducked. Sara screamed and yelled and then she collapsed in a heap and cried. I held her hand, my tears dropping onto her black hair. I could hear sniffs around the room. Sara's mother died of cancer. Sara's an orphan now. Her dad's been gone forever and she is living with foster parents until they find relatives to take her. She's only twelve. I never wanted a sister. It's bad enough having to put up with David and share everything with him but something about Sara gets to me. She's like a little black kitten with those pansy blue eyes. Anyway, watching Sara explode like that made me remember what I was going through a few months ago.

I love my journal. Maggie told us to write in it when we feel like it and to just put down whatever comes into our minds. Kind of let all the garbage spill out. It's sort of like that too. I pick up my pen and words come pouring off the end. It wasn't like that at first though. It was such an effort. I used to take a black marker and draw crosses over and over. There weren't any thoughts in my head, just feelings. Now I look forward to my writing time. I prop myself up on my yellow cushions on the window seat, the big old magnolia tree right on the other side of the glass. I open my journal, and memories, images flood into my mind. The best part is that Maggie says not to worry about punctuation or spelling, just write. No exam! Sometimes I read parts to the group but not very often. I'm surprised now when I see how much I've written and I realize how much time has passed. Maggie asked us yesterday to give one word to describe how we feel when we've finished our day's entry. I said, "calm." Other people answered, "relaxed," "sad," "rested," "drained." I've already mentioned Sara's response.

I lie in bed, admiring my re-decorated room. The ceiling and three walls are creamy white. The third wall is a bright lime green. My duvet cover is white with an abstract design stitched in purple. The photo of Jake and me on our bikes, from last summer, is the only thing on my picture board. I have to work on that. I've got some posters of the UBC campus. I'll put them up tomorrow. Each night now, I lie in bed and plan to do one special thing the next day. I visualize, dream, and drift off to sleep.

I'm steaming down Front Street on my Nishiki. The wind feels good on my face. I take the hill without standing up. I'm cruising down toward the river. I put one hand in my pocket; with the other I wave to the kids in the park.

Even before I open my eyes this morning, I can smell magnolias. I run to the window and see the enormous blooms — a white and purple canopy. It's spring again. There's that freshness in the air that I love. David is blasting out heavy metal. I'm going to get down to breakfast before he does.

Jake, is it okay if I feel happy again? Is it okay if I eat two eggs, toast and Mom's grape jelly for breakfast? Is it okay if I've got plans for today that I'm excited about? I'm going shopping with Josie and Cara for a graduation dress. Later I have to give Billy an answer about the dance. He asked me to go with him. It's hard without you but most days I can still see your face. I know you're here. I'm not saying good-bye, I'm just asking, is it okay?

Contributors' Notes

. . .

ASPIN, DIANA. *Cold Snap*

Diana Aspin writes short stories, poems and travel essays, and is presently working on her first novel. She wrote her first book at age six and sold it door-to-door. Her first "real" book, *Ordinary Miracles,* was published fifty-two years later and was nominated by the Canadian Library Association as one of the best ten books for young adults published that year. (This proves that it is never too late to write a book.) "Cold Snap" is one of Diana's favourite stories. As she was in the midst of writing the story, she remembers suddenly finding herself in the grip of the narrator's stunning anger and that anger propelling the story to its conclusion. Diana has worked as a civil servant, office cleaner, waitress, writing instructor, shop assistant, accounting clerk, receptionist, photographer (for travel writing) but best of all she worked at raising three kids — which was the most demanding work of all. More stories, two of them horror, will be published in Canadian anthologies in 2005–2006. Tips for wannabe writers? Read like there is no tomorrow. Write the same way. Let it be straight from the heart. Write to please yourself. Don't be afraid of the scary stuff that comes up — as story material it rocks!

ELLIS, SARAH. *Sisters*

Sarah Ellis spent a lot of her childhood under tables. She created, for example, her first (and last) graphic novel with a pencil on the underside of the family dining room table. She enjoyed reading, snacking, drawing and watching tv from under the table. Most of all she enjoyed listening. Sarah knew a lot of old people when she was a child and she noticed that old people have stories. She also noticed that people forget about a child who is under the table. One of her favourite places to visit was the home of two elderly neighbours who were sisters. Sarah didn't know that all the time she was sitting under their table listening, half-hidden by their lace tablecloth, she was in training to be a writer. She didn't know that years later, after both sisters had died, she would take out their stories and rearrange them into a story of her own. Sarah doesn't fit under tables any longer.

She has arranged a life that combines being a librarian and a writer. She has written picture books, juvenile novels, non-fiction and short stories. Her work has been translated into various languages and has won several awards such as the Mr. Christie Book Award, the Governor General's Award and the Sheila A. Egoff prize. She writes book reviews and speeches and has talked to children in every province in Canada. When she's not writing, she cooks, gardens, plays the ukulele and goes for long walks. Sometimes she gets too busy and has to remind herself to stop, hide, make believe and eavesdrop. She has to remind herself that it all starts under the table.

GAMACHE, DONNA. *Dear Family* —
Donna Gamache was born and raised in rural Manitoba. She attended university at Brandon, graduating with a Bachelor of Arts followed by an Education course. For a number of years she taught full time at the secondary level, then later as a part-time substitute. She is married with three grown sons. Donna has been writing professionally for many years. She has one published novel for children — *Spruce Woods Adventure* — and has published shorter items extensively for both adults and young people. Her short stories for children have been published in many Canadian and American magazines, such as *Cricket, On the Line, Kids' World, My Friend, and Short Story International.* For adults, her short stories have won several awards and have been

published in various anthologies, as well as *Western People, Our Family* and the *Toronto Sunday Star*. Non-fiction credits include articles in *Farmers Independent Weekly, Western People, Our Family, Canadian Author, Ski Trax* and others. She also publishes book reviews for *Prairie Fire Magazine* (on-line version), and short poetry for a number of publications. Recently she has taught several classes in writing fiction to both adults and children. Besides reading and writing, Donna enjoys a variety of outdoor activities, particularly camping, bird-watching, cross-country skiing, and riding her mountain bike.

About her story "Dear Family — " Gamache notes, "It was written using my usual method of plotting a story: the 'what if' method. I began by thinking, 'What if a woman left her family and moved away, in order to find herself? How would she react? How would her family react? What if they happened to meet again several years later?' I soon realized that this story should be told from the daughter's viewpoint. I decided to make the meeting a deliberate visit, an attempt by the daughter to understand her mother's leaving and to bridge the gap between them."

HEGERAT, BETTY JANE. *Kick*
Betty Jane Hegerat is a Calgary fiction writer, a social worker by profession, and an occasional teacher of creative writing at the Alexandra Writers' Centre. Her short stories have been published in literary magazines and broadcast

on CBC radio. Her first novel, *Running Toward Home,* will be published by NeWest Press in the fall of 2006. "Kick" is the first story she has written specifically for a young audience, although she finds herself frequently writing adult fiction from the perspective of young people Justin's age. *Running Toward Home,* while it is an adult novel, is also the story of a twelve-year-old boy.

"Kick" was born of the experience some years ago of one of her own children when an elementary school classmate was killed in a traffic accident. With all of the best intentions, the school provided a counsellor for the whole class. What was a sad event and a harsh lesson in vulnerability, became even more of an emotional upheaval. The child who barely knew the victim came away feeling guilty that he could not summon the sadness he was "supposed" to feel. The storyteller took the situation a step farther with the perennial "what if . . . ?" What if the child not only had barely known the dead classmate, but had actively disliked him? What if the boy who died was a bully? How does his victim deal with the sense that his own dark wishes have come true?

KELLER, JESSIE MAY. *Balance Restored*
Jessie May Keller is a retired teacher who lives with her husband in Vancouver. She begins most mornings with a long walk in Pacific Spirit Park. Her interests include gardening, tapestry weaving, reading and playing on Wednesday morn-

ings with her twin grandchildren. She enjoys travelling. Some memorable trips include bicycling the Oregon coast, canoeing on the Yukon river and hiking the Coast-to-Coast trail in England. May's early years were spent with her seven siblings in a log house in the Okanagan where her first classroom was a one-room schoolhouse. At twenty, May had completed three years of psychiatric nurse's training. She has a teaching degree (M.Ed.) from the University of British Columbia and has spent most of her career working with children with behavioural and/or emotional problems. Recently, May completed a diploma course in writing for children and teenagers with the Institute of Children's Literature.

"Balance Restored" is a short story about the various stages of grieving. The process of grieving is a private matter. Each individual grieves in his/her own way; there is no right or wrong way. The five stages of grieving (Denial, Anger, Bargaining, Depression and Acceptance) have been adapted from the pioneering work and writings of Elizabeth Kubler-Ross. Not all people experience each stage; neither do they necessarily go through the stages in order. Although Alexandra in the story appears to benefit from counselling, recent studies suggest that not all individuals require this. Like Alexandra, many children are resilient: they can experience trauma, come to terms with it, and eventually achieve balance. Caring, supportive people in their lives are essential.

KENNEDY, LIBBY. *Dreams in a Pizza Box*

Libby Kennedy has won several prizes for short fiction in the Cecilia Lamont and the Bard's Ink competitions. She spends her time writing children's stories and works of creative non-fiction for adults. She is currently working on a collection of short stories for women. Libby has the following to say about her story: "The story had its origin in an event that occurred in the middle of a cold Alberta winter. A woman pushes a shopping cart through a snow-covered alley in Calgary. By her side is a little girl. A grey toque can barely contain her blonde curls; over-sized gloves and rubber boots cannot possibly keep her warm. The mother plucks a half-eaten ice cream cone from a dumpster behind a fast food restaurant and hands it to the child. The little girl beams as if she has just received the most incredible gift in the world. I dedicate 'Dreams In A Pizza Box' to this little girl — I hope you are well. I hope you are warm. In addition, I would like to thank my mother and the many volunteers at the food bank. Your work is truly selfless: you nourish with food, respect and dignity."

LOHANS, ALISON. *A Few Words for My Brother*

Alison Lohans has witnessed the impact of Fetal Alcohol Spectrum Disorder (FASD) first-hand. This entirely preventable disease — for which there is no known cure — has touched the lives of countless individuals. Alcohol consumption during pregnancy can produce irreversible brain damage in the fetus. Some manifestations of FASD include Attention Deficit Hyperactive Disorder (ADHD), impulsive behaviour, and an inability to link actions with their consequences. Sadly, some young people who are affected by this disability end up in serious trouble with the law.

Alison has been writing all her life and was first published at the age of twelve. She has published thirteen books for young adults and children, as well as numerous short stories, poems and nonfiction pieces. Most of her books have appeared on the Canadian Children's Book Centre "Our Choice" list, and many have been contenders for awards. Some of these include *Don't Think Twice, Foghorn Passage, Laws of Emotion, Waiting for the Sun* and *Nathaniel's Violin.* Her books have been translated into French, Swedish, and Norwegian. Alison has given hundreds of author talks and writing workshops at schools, libraries and conferences across Canada, and was Writer-in-Residence at Regina Public Library in 2002–2003. She does occasional teaching, and some of her students have won awards for their writing. Alison Lohans lives in Regina. In her spare time, she enjoys playing in musical groups, reading, gardening and taking classes in watercolour. Her fourteenth book, *The Raspberry Room,* will be published in 2006.

MAC, CARRIE. *the sign for heaven*
Carrie Mac is a Vancouver-based writer who was raised in small-town British Columbia, where there is no shortage of

interesting people to spy on, should a small four-eyed curious child have the notion to do so. When she discovered that spies were expected to keep quiet about what they observe and weren't supposed to tell tall tales, she decided she'd be a writer instead. This was before she understood things like "annual income," and the need for one. Ever-determined, she had her first book in the Grand Forks Public Library system when she was six. Mind you, it was stapled together and had lots of simple words written in crayon and scrawly pictures, but it had its very own index card and had to be signed out like any other book, much to her delight. At age twenty-five, she was awarded a Canada Council for the Arts Grant for her novel *The Beckoners,* which has won the Arthur Ellis YA award, is a CLA Honour book, and has been optioned for film. She is also the author of *Charmed,* and has had numerous short stories published in a variety of snooty literary journals. She is currently juggling two novels and a short story collection and a paramedic license (she now understands what "annual income" means). It's probably best not to mention her screenplays, both of which skulk around whispering nasty things at her in the dead of night. The poor things, they're just desperate for attention.

About "the sign for heaven," she comments: "I've always had a fascination with death and dying, but that seems logical to me, since death is the end of life, and I find life endlessly fascinating, too. However, I seem to have had more than my fair share of dead people in my life, which has given me lots of opportunity to ponder the Big Questions — which I highly recommend doing. I dearly and still miss the people I've lost, but I'm also thankful for what each of their lives and deaths has taught me about life and loss and love and grief. My story 'the sign for heaven' is based on my friendship with a little girl who died when I was thirteen. That same year, another close friend of mine was murdered, and shortly after that, my grandpa — who was like a father to me — also died. It was definitely a dark time for me, but as humans on this planet, we all have dark times, and that's okay, because it's all a part of being alive in the first place, which is a blessing."

MARACLE, LEE. *The Canoe*

Lee Maracle is a member of the Sto:lo nation. She was born in North Vancouver, is the mother of four and grandmother of four. She has a number of books to her name, including *Ravensong, Will's Garden* (a young adult novel), *Sojourners & Sundogs, I Am Woman* and *Daughters are Forever.* She is also the co-editor of a number of anthologies, including the award-winning *My Home As I Remember.* In addition, she is published in a number of anthologies and has done a great deal of editing work. She is currently the First Nations Writer in Residence at the University of Toronto.

In discussing the background of "The Canoe," Maracle notes: "A great many Native people suffer the death of one parent or another while they are still teenagers. When it is the mother, the fathers sometimes have a very hard time dealing with it because traditionally the children 'belong to the mother' and the fathers don't interfere much with the raising and teaching of the children. Although in 'The Canoe' the father seems angry at the son in the beginning, in the end he is upset with himself. Anger over loss is like that, it feels as if you are angry at everyone, but really, you are upset with your own shortcomings and sad about your loss. I lived for a short time on the west coast of Vancouver Island among the Nuu-chah-nulth people and this story is to honour their kindness to me."

McCOWAN, PATRICIA. *Hang On*

Patricia McCowan grew up in Winnipeg, where she earned her BA in Theatre and Drama from the University of Winnipeg and studied acting at the Banff Centre School of Fine Arts. She now lives with her husband and two daughters in Toronto, where she is the librarian at her oldest daughter's school. Her short story "The Bike" was shortlisted in the 2004 Writers' Union of Canada's Writing for Children contest. "Hang On" is her first published work.

Patricia has the following to say about "Hang On": "It did not start out being a story about loss. It started with an image in my head of a painting — the blue 'Moonlight' painting Randy's parents hang above their piano. Then I pictured a boy looking at this painting and hating it, and I wanted to discover why he hated it. So off I went with Kevin. Kevin and Randy live in the landscapes of kitchens and convenience stores, back doors and parking lots, and a rain-slicked rail-crossing in an ignored part of town. They smell the landscape and feel it, they hear the noises in it, and move through it. Kevin and Randy's landscape is alive to them in a way the decorative 'landscape' paintings, safely contained in fancy frames on the Krawchuks' walls, can never be. After the accident, the happiness of that shared place — singing goofy songs on their bikes, throwing pennies on the tracks — will be a thing of the past for Kevin. He may be losing not only Randy, but the landscape of their friendship as well. So the moonlit painting of 'the empty ship that would never leave the harbour' and 'the buildings that would always be dark' can evoke nothing but anger in Kevin. It is a landscape without life. But even though 'Hang On' became a story about loss, I hope that, with Kevin's ability to 'almost laugh' at the end, it is also a story about hanging on to what remains alive."

POGUE, CAROLYN. *Snow Angel*
Calgary author Carolyn Pogue writes fiction and nonfiction for young readers and adults. One of her previous stories, "To Begin Again," was published in the Ronsdale anthology *Beginnings* edited by Ann Walsh. Other stories and articles have been published in magazines such as *Canadian Living, Synchronicity, Legacy, The United Church Observer* and

Alberta Views. For many years Carolyn has joined other authors as writer-in-residence at YouthWrite, a summer camp for writers aged twelve to eighteen, which takes place in the Rocky Mountains. In 2004 she was "peace-writer-in-residence" at Provost Public School, Alberta. Carolyn is the author of seven books. Her most recent is *A New Day: Peacemaking Stories and Activities* (UCPH, 2005). In September 2005, *Remember Peace,* a book for teachers, will be published by Connections Publishing International. Carolyn is a peace activist who helped start a Calgary branch of the peace group, Women in Black. Carolyn has travelled in many countries of the world, and has lived in Ontario, Quebec and Northwest Territories. You can learn more at www.carolynpogue.ca.

Carolyn says of "Snow Angel": "It is a story like a patchwork quilt. It is made with a patch of fiction and a patch of nonfiction, a patch of colour and then one of black and white, a patch of memory and a patch of hope. The idea for it came when I began thinking about snow angels and how, even after they disappear, they can live in our memories. Elizabeth Ann is a made-up character and completely fictitious. But Elizabeth Ann is also real; she is very much like Kathryn Ann, who at one time lived and loved and is now buried at Lakeview Cemetery in Yellowknife, Northwest Territories. Like Elizabeth Ann, Kathryn Ann's life was difficult because, when her mother was pregnant, she drank alcohol. Like Elizabeth Ann, Kathryn Ann died when she was young, but she still lives in the memories of the family that loved her. There is nothing fictitious about Fetal Alcohol Syndrome (FAS) and Fetal Alcohol Effect (FAE). About one thousand babies affected by alcohol are born in Canada each year. If you think you might be pregnant, or might become pregnant, stay away from this poison. Once I saw a picture of the brain of an FAS child. It had holes in it. No one can fix this brain; children born with FAS face more difficulties than other kids. I dedicate this story to all brave children who struggle because their birth mothers drank alcohol or took drugs. This story was written in memory of Kathryn Ann Marie, 1979–1993."

ROZON, GINA. *Explaining Andrew*
Given the dark tone of "Explaining Andrew," it may come as a surprise for readers to learn that Gina Rozon is a humour columnist. Her self-syndicated column appears in newspapers serving over five hundred rural communities in Saskatchewan and aired on CBC Radio Saskatchewan from 2001 to 2003. Her humour has also appeared in the anthology *North by North Wit,* in *Stitches Magazine,* and in *Reader's Digest (Canada).* "Explaining Andrew," a story that began as a writing exercise at a meeting of the La Ronge Wild Rice Writers' Group, appeared for the first time in the Canadian Mental Health Association's literary magazine, *Transition,* in 2003. As a result of her experience as an apprentice in the 2005 Saskatchewan Writers' Guild Men-

torship Program, Gina is currently working on completing a novel based on material from her columns. Born and raised in Port Alberni, B.C., Gina has lived in La Ronge, Saskatchewan, with her husband and two children, since 1997. You will find further information at www.ginarozon. com.

WALSH, ANN. *All is Calm*

Ann Walsh is the author of six novels for young readers, most set during the B.C. gold rush. In addition, Ann is the author of a book of poetry and has edited three collections of short stories. She also writes for adult readers and her work has appeared in magazines and anthologies around the world. In Canada, her articles have been published in the *Vancouver Sun, Canadian Living* and *Arts Forum.* They have also been heard on CBC radio. Ann is a popular workshop presenter at conferences for young writers and is in demand as a speaker, both in schools and at literary festivals. Her books have been nominated for major Canadian book prizes, and all of them have been selected as "Our Choice" titles by the Canadian Children's Book Centre.

In thinking about the writing of her story "All is Calm," Ann notes: "Almost half a million Canadian seniors have Alzheimer's disease or another type of dementia. That's about one in thirteen. After the age of eighty-five, the number goes up to one in three. More than half the population of Canada knows someone with the disease; almost a quarter of us has a relative suffering from dementia. My family is one of the twenty-five percent who have been affected by Alzheimer's. When my mother-in-law was in the early stages of the disease, my oldest daughter was a university student in the city where Mum lived. Katherine did what she could to help. She took Mum to doctor's appointments, reminded her to eat, to take her medicine and to pay her bills. Although 'All is Calm' is fiction, the idea for it began with Katie and her grandmother. The pain of being forgotten by someone you love is unlike any other pain. You feel invisible, unwanted, unloved. There is nothing you can do but cry, not just for yourself but for the person who is slowly losing her memories. Because when people lose their memories, they lose themselves — everything they are, everything they love, every dream and every hope they once had. Alzheimer's is one of Nature's most heartbreaking diseases. This story is for everyone who is going through that heartbreak. It is dedicated in loving memory to Frances Walsh."

About *Dark Times*

This anthology was compiled from more than two hundred submissions from across Canada, and would not have been possible without the encouragement and support of Veronica and Ronald Hatch of Ronsdale Press. Thank you both for your gentle guidance and thoughtful advice.

— ANN WALSH